W9-DJE-240

COPING
W I T H

Being
Gifted

Being
Gifted

Sharon Carter and

Lawrence Clayton

THE ROSEN PUBLISHING GROUP, INC. NEW YORK

8 -22 - 96

Published in 1992 by The Rosen Publishing Group, Inc.
29 East 21st Street, New York, NY 10010

First Edition

Library of Congress Cataloging-in-Publication Data

Carter, Sharon.
    Coping with being gifted / S. Carter and L. Clayton.—1st ed.

        p.   cm.
    Includes bibliographical references and index.
    Summary: A discussion of how to cope with some of the problems of being a teenager of special ability, including problems with friendships, family relationships, and how to use a gift for the best.
    ISBN 0-8239-1430-5
    1. Gifted children—United States—Juvenile literature.
[1. Gifted children.]   I. Clayton, L. (Lawrence)   II. Title.
HQ773.5.C37   1992
305.23′0879—dc20   91-35231
                                                                CIP
                                                                AC

Manufactured in the United States of America

To my siblings:
Grace, Diane, and Rick
Each of whom possesses
His own unique
Gift

Lawrence Clayton

ABOUT THE AUTHORS ◇

Sharon Carter is a free-lance writer, living in Oklahoma City. Part Choctaw Indian, she was born on a Sioux Reservation in North Dakota, where her father was a teacher. Later she herself taught on a Navajo Reservation in New Mexico.

On magazine and newspaper assignments she has raced stock cars, ridden many lights-and-siren ambulance calls, raced sailboats, flown with a Police Department helicopter, and appeared on national TV. A licensed pilot, she has flown aircraft that include hot air balloons, helicopters, World War II fighters, the Goodyear blimp, and an Oklahoma Air National Guard jet fighter.

Lawrence Clayton grew up in a small mining town in central Nevada. A gifted child who had a learning disorder, he experienced firsthand the multifaceted dynamics common to such children.

Joining the United States Army at seventeen, he eventually served three years in Germany and two years in Vietnam. He completed a high school equivalency diploma (GED) while in the service. Later he earned a bachelor's degree (summa cum laude) from Texas Wesleyan College, Fort Worth. After graduate work at Emory University, where he received the Dean's Award, he earned a master's degree at Texas Christian University and a doctorate at Texas Woman's University (the graduate school is coeducational).

Dr. Clayton has specialized in treating children, youth, and families as an ordained minister, a certified drug and alcohol counselor, and a clinical marriage and family therapist. He founded and directs the Oklahoma Family Institute, a Christian counseling center in Oklahoma City.

Other books by Dr. Clayton include *Assessment and Management of the Suicidal Adolescent*, *Coping with Depression*, *Coping with Drug-Abusing Parents*, and *Careers in Psychology*. He also is Associate Editor of the journal *Family Perspective*.

Dr. Clayton lives with his wife, Cathy, and their three children, Rebecca, Larry, and Amy, in Piedmont, Oklahoma.

Contents

CHAPTER 1

"Gifted"—What Exactly Does It Mean?

According to Webster's *New Collegiate Dictionary*, the word *gifted* means "having great natural ability." According to the general public, if you are gifted you are simply smarter than the average bear. In the "gifted and talented" programs of most schools, that is the standard used to judge who gets in. If, say, your IQ is 130, you automatically go into the category known as "gifted."

That does explain "gifted," but we feel it falls short. Being gifted is much more than that.

You are gifted if you have a special ability in any field. You may be a whiz at math or have a real flair for writing. Perhaps music is your thing. Or science. Or athletics.

Whatever, you are gifted if your ability and skills in one particular area are beyond those of most people your age.

You are usually aware of that "specialness" about yourself, that you are unique and that you will be a success in life. Some people say they knew as early as age four or five that they were different, somehow special and marked for success.

We believe that girls tend to have a better understanding of their giftedness than do boys. Girls—and women—seem to understand themselves, as well as other people, better than the male half of the species *Homo sapiens* do. That may explain why, so often, a boy who was nothing special academically in grade school suddenly gets his act together in middle or high school and makes the honor roll and academic stardom from there on.

According to the male half of this writing team, little boys get much more encouragement to act "tough and dumb" in grade school than to display any special brain power. That encouragement comes from many sources—television, radio, movies, family, and books. It is enforced by peers who are receiving the same impetus from the same sources.

A person can have one or more learning disorders, some of them even serious, and still be gifted. That is not even unusual. In fact, it's rather common. Often the learning disorders tend to hide the giftedness. Only the sharpest teacher or parent may be able to see past the disorder and recognize the person's special strengths, abilities, and talents.

We believe that labeling a school program as being for the "gifted and talented" is redundant. Being gifted, above average, in any field is the same as being talented.

Unfortunately, selection of students for such programs is usually done on the basis of IQ only.

We believe that sometimes overlooks some of the best prospects—kids who may be outstanding in one or two areas but not across-the-board brilliant. For example, it would miss someone who can write like Richard Peck, S.E. Hinton, or Judy Blume but whose math score is so lousy that it pulls other scores down to the "average" category. (Or vice versa.) Such kids are gifted, occasionally even brilliant, in one special field but not in everything.

Selection of "talent" becomes a judgment call, and one that has been known to ruffle feathers. It is not at all uncommon to hear the complaint, "If you play a band instrument well or classical piano even halfway well, you're automatically in the gifted and talented classes. If you play rock and roll or sing country and western, forget it. They won't even consider you."

The complainers have a definite point. It is not recognition of musical talent but plain snobbism that is making the determination.

The judgment call happens in athletics as well. "Dumb jock" has become a cliché. It is really an extension of the idea that boys are supposed to act "dumb and tough," and it can follow the brightest and most gifted athlete right into adulthood.

Ask any football player, from high school to the NFL, how often he has been treated as if his IQ were not quite as high as the average room temperature. Plenty of times, he'll almost certainly tell you.

(In matters of learning and intellectual achievement, this academics vs. athletics issue takes a different twist. When a college team is in the top ten or even top twenty in the nation, or up for a national or even a conference championship, you are likely to hear some of the professors *at that college* complain that the athletic program is "ruining" the university, that they ought to drop the program and concentrate on scholastics, that most athletes don't have brains enough to tie their own shoes, and so on.

(According to the Athletic Department at the University of Oklahoma, whose basketball and football teams both did it in the same year, whenever you have a team going up for a national championship it increases by about 4,000 the number of high school seniors who apply for admission. OU is in the top five public schools in the nation in attracting National Merit Scholarship students—but *that* you don't hear the professors griping about!)

The point is, no matter how well you know that you are gifted, that you are special, that you are going to succeed, it may not be recognized by the people at school, or at home for that matter. It may be that recognizing and making the most of your special ability is mainly up to you.

That can take a great deal of dedication, because bucking the expectations of school, church, family, and friends can be like walking a tightrope with your hands tied behind you. But gifted people are exactly the ones to do it.

We think that too many parents don't pay enough attention to their children's special abilities. Typically, when a kid brings home a report card with four As and one C, you know where the focus of attention is going to be.

Of course.

Can't you just hear it? "C in English! How in thunder could a kid get a C in English? I know—you spend so much time in front of the TV and you just *don't study!*"

The big problem is that, faced with attitudes like that at home and indifference at school, a lot of kids lose that belief in their own specialness, their own ability.

Mention of this book project brought raised eyebrows among friends and general reactions along the lines of, "*Coping* with being gifted? What's to cope, being smarter than other people? Seems to me those kids have it made."

As any of you reading this know, being gifted is a blessing, but it is by no means an unmixed one. There are a lot of things you *do* have to cope with, a lot of problems that come your way because of your ability or your talent. They are problems that other kids don't have and often would never even guess exist.

Keep reading. That's what this book is all about.

CHAPTER 2

Talent vs. Common Sense

Gene is an adult now, a former NASA aeronautical engineer who is finishing his Ph.D. so he can teach other rocket scientists. He is a brilliant, successful man with a great marriage, children who have never caused any problems, and a good life all the way around.

"Try telling that to some of my relatives," he says, with a half-grin, half-sigh. "Do you know how a lot of them see me, even now? Mention me and they'll tell you about the time when I was twelve. I had always been totally fascinated by anything that flew and how it flew. Out of an old parachute, some light metal poles, and wooden strips I built this 'flying machine'—gliding machine, really. It was basically a pair of rigid wings strapped to my back. I put them on and jumped off the roof of my grandfather's barn. The wings flew for just a minute, then fell off to one side and I crashed and burned on the spot. I broke my arm in two places.

"I got about a year-long chewing out for that, from my folks, grandparents, and assorted aunts, uncles, and other relatives. It wasn't until years later that I learned what had happened. Some cousins, who had always been jealous of me because I made better grades, played sports, and things like that, stuffed some rocks into the metal tubes on one side. The cousin who told me about it was laughing like a hyena—and I decked him on the spot.

"I went back after that—I was in college by then—and rebuilt those wings and they worked, even though I was a lot bigger and heavier by then. It was a primitive form of hang glider, but they *did* work. Yet mention my name to a lot of my relatives and I know what they'll say. 'Oh, Gene's smart in some ways, all right. He just doesn't have any common sense.'"

Lynn runs a fingernail down a crease in a clipping from the *New York Times*. The story carries her byline. Beside her are a stack of magazines—*Vogue, Cosmopolitan, Mademoiselle*. All of them contain articles by her.

"I always wanted to be a writer. Ever since I found out it was people who made stories and books and that they didn't just generate by some sort of magic. I always made up stories and told them to my sisters and other kids. We could do and be almost anything—I made us have the most wonderful adventures. It was tremendous fun. And I suppose sometimes my imagination did run away with me—it does with most kids now and again.

"Do you know what the reaction was, not so much from my parents, but a lot of my other relatives? 'Boy, you have got the wildest imagination!' Always in an accusing sort of way.

"Of course I had a vivid imagination! How could I make

anything real to anyone else if I couldn't make it real to me? But the way they said it, it was a put-down. Always a put-down. Something wrong with me. Why couldn't I be like this cousin, or that one? They had good 'common sense.' Their imagination didn't get the upper hand.

"Even after I began to be pretty widely published, pretty well known in my field, I still heard that. I got snide remarks about my imagination from one particular aunt until the end of her life, as if imagination were a character defect that, unless controlled and repressed, would one day get me jailed!"

Jerry, as a kid, always wanted to know why. He wanted to understand how things worked. When he heard the biblical story of creation, he immediately asked, "If God made everything, who made God?" and "If Adam and Eve and their children were the only ones alive, why does it say that Cain moved away to live in a city? And where did Cain and Abel get their wives?"

His grandfather became very angry and bellowed, "You must never question God! Don't you know what a terrible thing that is?" Jerry made himself very unpopular in his rigidly fundamentalist family.

In high school Jerry asked the same kinds of questions about his father's retirement fund. "What would happen if the fund's investments were poor? Would you lose all your money? Come on, Dad, face it. The company's track record of money management hasn't been all that great lately." His father became angry and yelled, "Don't you question the company! It has fed and clothed and taken pretty good care of us for almost twenty years!"

But Jerry kept asking questions until finally his father listened, added up a few facts, and got his money out of the company retirement fund just before it was declared bankrupt.

Today Jerry is a popular, successful defense attorney. But a lot of his friends from earlier days still remember him as the kid who dared to question God and brought down the wrath of his grandfather.

The young Russian boy came from poor, uneducated parents in a remote Russian village. His grandfather, moreover, had disgraced and endangered the family by serving a nine-year term in the *gulag* (prison) under the regime of Joseph Stalin. The families of anyone who had served time in the *gulag* were lucky to get even the most menial jobs.

Mikhail's classmates wanted to be truck drivers, farmers, mechanics. One day in class he was asked what he would like to be and he replied, "A diplomat." The whole class laughed—including the teacher. Pigs had a better chance of flying seemed to be the consensus. He had better concentrate on something that showed common sense, like learning to farm or tend livestock.

Yet Mikhail had a flair for diplomacy, even at a young age. A few days later, in German class, a flap occurred when the teacher asked them to sing, in German, a song about the then deeply honored, almost God-like Lenin. The song contained the word *führer*. This was just after World War II, and the Germans were hated in Russia. The whole class, as Bart Simpson might put it, had a cow. To them *führer* meant Hitler. How could anyone ask them to sing about Hitler and their beloved Lenin in the same song?

Mikhail picked up a German-Russian dictionary and passed it around to his classmates. "See?" he said calmly, pointing. *"Führer* just means 'leader.' Any leader."

The class got back to their song.

The boy was Mikhail Gorbachev, who went on to become a diplomat who literally changed the world.

Why do you hear about common sense so often where brighter than average people are concerned?

Gene hit on what we think is one of the key reasons—jealousy. A lot of people realize that you have an edge on them, an advantage, something they don't have.

You may be smarter BUT. Put-downs here mean exactly what put-downs mean in any other situation.

The person putting you down is hoping you'll be at least at his level.

Smarter is smarter. Smarter people have more success in life, better marriages, better relationships with others.

We believe the "You have no common sense" cliché comes from two basic sources.

First, it is not what you *don't* have that causes other people problems, but what you *do* have. Like Gene, Lynn, Jerry, and Mikhail, you see and imagine and envision a dozen possibilities that other kids would never come up with in their wildest dreams.

Gene built a working hang glider before the general public had ever heard of such a thing. Except for the sabotage, it would have flown.

Other kids had access to as many words as Lynn, but her talent enabled her to string those words together in a way that made people want to read them.

Jerry would not just accept things. He wanted to know why, and he saw possibilities that other people were too blind, or too complacent, to see.

Mikhail saw beyond his small village, uneducated

parents, and "criminal" grandfather and realized that he could succeed at what he wanted to do in life.

The gifted kid is the five-year-old who sticks a hairpin in a light socket after being told not to, not because he is dumb but because "You'll get shocked" doesn't mean anything to him. Mom was shocked at some language on TV, and Grandma is shocked by his sister's lying in the sun in her bikini. "Shocked" doesn't make any sense in this connection. He has to find out for himself.

This is also the kid who takes the alarm clock apart and rewires it so it makes the telephone ring. Many parents and other adults are exasperated at the destruction of the alarm clock, the possible damage to the telephone, and the general unheaval around the house. They don't see the inquiring mind behind it, the drive to *know*, to experiment, to explore the possibilities.

The second source of the "no common sense" cliché is not that you are lacking anything, but that in other areas you are just average or maybe a bit below average. You excel in one or some areas, but not in everything. People whose special area is the one where you don't exactly shine may jump to the conclusion that you are goofing off, not really trying—not working at it as someone with "common sense" would do.

David has never made less than an A in math. In his entire life! He is a computer whiz whose work, according to his teacher, is advanced college level. He speaks good English, but to him the inner workings of the language make about as much sense as misspelled romantic poetry written in Outer Mongolian shorthand.

"We got into this 'diagram a sentence' garbage," he says,

in a despairing voice. "Man, that stuff . . . anyway, the teacher drew this sprawled out mess on the blackboard that looked like someone had swatted a giant spider, and she starts asking me this and that about it and getting mad when I can't tell her. Look, I can memorize what the book says as well as the next guy, but when you get away from what the book says, I'm lost. I can't make it connect up in my mind. It just doesn't make *sense* to me.

"Well, when I can't give her the right answers, the teacher starts getting mad. I have a reputation around school for being pretty smart, you know. In some classes I get real good grades without much effort. So she thinks I'm not trying in her class, or maybe being sarcastic or something. She chews me up one side and down the other and ends up practically yelling that I don't have any 'common sense.'

"Look, I make Bs and Cs in her class, but she's not satisfied with that. Because I'm good in math she's giving me blazes because I'm not good at junk like diagramming sentences. How can I be good at something when I don't basically *understand*—either it, or what good it could possibly do you?"

David has a very valid point, which is discussed in a later chapter. Here the fault lies with the teacher.

Teachers *and* parents are too likely to think that being gifted in one area means being gifted in all. Actually that is pretty rare, certainly rarer than having special ability in one or two fields. So you may be getting a lot of pressure to excel in something for which you really have little ability.

We mentioned math earlier. That is a common hang-up. A student who makes mostly As but in math is relieved to squeak through with a C is very likely to hear, as David did, "If you just *studied* harder . . .," "If you just applied yourself . . .," "You get good grades in everything else. Why do you have to goof off in algebra?"

You can't do it because you can't. The ability simply is not there. If you are nagged on the point long enough, you may begin to give up, not to care so much about getting good grades in other classes, or to buy the negative view of yourself and decide that maybe you aren't so smart after all.

Carla, fourteen, had always made good grades, although arithmetic was a struggle, until the family moved and she started going to a new school where her aunt was vice principal—and her math teacher.

"I knew I had a hard time with anything to do with numbers," Carla said. "Well, when I started at this school and got in Aunt Cora's class, it went from hard to miserable. She knew I made good grades in every other class, and she was on my case all the time because I wasn't doing well in algebra. She kept telling me I would need it in later life. Man, I can't imagine how!

"Anyway, she said I wasn't doing well because I wasn't studying. I couldn't convince her that I put in twice as much time on her class as all the others combined."

Because she was spending so much time on algebra, Carla's other grades began to slip. And because she was constantly being harassed about her problems in that one class, she began to slip into such a state of depression that she found it hard to concentrate on other classes, even those she liked and normally did well in.

By the end of that school year Carla had gone from being an honor roll student to one with a C average. And according to Aunt Cora, it was every bit Carla's fault.

Nobody could have made Aunt Cora see that *she* was the culprit behind most of Carla's problems.

This, we think, is where the Soviet school system has some aspects that are superior to our own. In the Soviet Union youngsters are individually tested and evaluated and receive schooling according to their special abilities— which might not even be academic ability.

If a child shows great athletic promise, he or she goes into special training as a shot putter, a gymnast, a skater, a dancer. No one cares if he or she cannot quote from the works of Tolstoy or Chekov. No one pressures him or her to learn calculus if he or she does not have a flair for it. The person is honored for the ability he or she *does* have.

Both the authors remember courses in graduate school that were *monsters*, in which we comprehended just a fraction of what was being taught. We managed to get the grades we needed, but it was the sort of experience that can lead to ulcers, gray hair, nails gnawed down to the first knuckle and—it seemed at times—incipient homicidal mania. So we certainly know how it feels to have a tough time with something.

Keep reading. We'll deal with such issues as jealousy and unwarranted pressure later on.

CHAPTER 3

"But Everyone Says I'm Dumb"

Steve, at fifteen, was a good kid whom most people liked and found fun to be around, but his parents and teachers had long ago decided that he just wasn't a scholar. His parents had accepted it and no longer nagged him about his mediocre grades. Then, one summer evening, several friends came to Steve's house for a cookout. Among the guests was the sister of a neighbor, a high school teacher in another state.

After dinner Steve came around the corner of the house from where the kids had been playing volley ball, to hear the adults talking as they sat on the patio.

"Yeah, Steve's a real good kid and has never caused us any problems," his mother was saying. "We've just gotten used to the fact that he's not college material and . . ."

"Why in the world do you say that?" the teacher asked, sounding surprised.

"Well—he tries. I mean, the poor kid studies and all that, but Cs and a very occasional B are about his limit."

"Now, that's really odd. Have you ever had Steve tested to see if he might have some kind of learning disability? Because if you asked me, I'd say he's not slower than the ordinary kid, I'd say he's *brighter* than average."

This caused quite a flap, and when the flurry of voices died down and the teacher was asked to explain, she said, "Why do I think so? Several reasons. For one, his sense of humor. You don't find that kind of humor in the dull-to-normal intelligence range. And his vocabulary. Just listen to the kid—he talks like a college student. Look, get the boy thoroughly evaluated. It's my guess you've got a very bright young man there, and it's all going to waste."

Steve edged away, "feeling like I'd been clipped by an iron pipe. I mean, everyone had always said I was dumb. I figured they were right. I didn't *feel* dumb, but I had such a hard time in school I figured I'd never be much more than a grocery sacker or spend my working life flipping burgers in a fast-food joint. I couldn't believe what I was hearing."

Steve's parents sent him to a learning disorders center that was part of a children's hospital in their city—and everyone was astonished at the results.

First, Steve needed glasses. He always did better when he sat in the front of a classroom, and he usually took a front seat when given a choice. But he was a quiet, easygoing kid, and teachers tended to move him to the back row, putting the troublemakers up front where they could keep an eye on them. Steve had had several eye tests, the "Stand here and read the lines on the chart" kind, but he had never been examined by an ophthalmologist. His visual problem was fairly unusual, one that would not be detected in a test by an untrained person. Once he had glasses, Steve said it was as if a whole new world opened up, the difference between night and day.

Second, he had a mild learning disorder. When he heard two separate sounds—for example, the teacher talking and a strong wind blowing outside—they blended together to become one meaningless blur of noise. That was why teachers and parents so often jumped on him for not paying attention. If there was a competing noise, he literally did not hear a word they said.

Third, Steve had a mild hearing loss in one ear, probably from a car accident when he was three. Even when there were no competing noises, he had trouble hearing everything said in class.

These problems were corrected to a large degree by allowing Steve to sit in a front-row seat where there were fewer sounds to compete for his attention to what the teacher was saying.

Tested again, Steve had an IQ of 128. His special strengths were in areas of science. He is now making almost straight As and thinking of becoming a doctor. To everyone who knows him, it seems like a miracle.

"Talk about feeling guilty!" his mother said. "We've really felt lower than worms about this. All the time we were selling Steve short. It never occurred to us that he couldn't see or hear. I knew he had eye exams at school, and I assumed they would catch any problem. When I think how often I had jumped all over him for not paying attention when he genuinely could not hear me, I figure I'll spend the rest of my life apologizing."

Laura had never wanted to be anything but a reporter. She started a kids' newspaper when she was ten, got her first byline in a city newspaper at twelve, and was a regular stringer (writer paid by the inch for stories she submitted that were published) by the time she was fourteen. Her heroine was Edna Buchanan, Pulitzer Prize–winning police reporter of the Miami *Herald*. An editor of the paper for which she worked as a stringer said, "You know, I think this kid might grow up to be one of the great ones."

But when Laura started high school she was evaluated and found to have a fairly marked dyslexia for numbers (the learning disorder in which numbers (or letters) are seen not in the order in which they exist, but as a confusing, sometimes even moving, jumble).

It didn't surprise her; she had never liked math or been very good at it. She knew she had to struggle hard in any class, or project, involving math.

In this school, however, the finding of dyslexia was all it took. Laura was placed in the Learning Disabled program across the board. Worse—journalism classes were electives that were not open to Learning Disabled or Special Ed kids.

Laura entered high school with enthusiasm, sure of her education and career goals, what she wanted in life. Now, thanks to the mindless and soulless bureaucracy we find too often in our society, she hates school passionately, is sick much of the time with headaches, stomach problems, and skin rashes, and has her parents threatening everything under the sun to keep her from dropping out of school.

Sherry was always very strong. Although small, she was stronger than many boys older than she.

Her mother was always nagging her to "Act like a lady!" But Sherry was a tomboy, happiest during the summer when she could help her father buck hay. She worked long and hard hours without complaint, with enjoyment.

School was another matter. Sherry struggled with every subject. She hated homework to the point that most nights saw a running battle between her and her mother. Her teachers were often angry with her. Finally, she flunked seventh grade.

Then her parents sold their farm and moved the family to another state. Sherry's new school routinely tested all new students, and when her evaluation came back everyone was surprised—even somewhat unbelieving.

Sherry had an IQ of 134, and she had superior gross motor skills, the kinds used in lifting, climbing, running, the things she most loved to do.

She also had very poor fine motor skills, for the small movements used in activities such as writing and reading. In fact, the school psychologist explained, "Just having to copy down the math problems is torture to Sherry, and reading a chapter in a book absolutely exhausts her."

The psychologist suggested that her books be tape recorded, so Sherry could listen to them rather than go through the strain of reading, and that her math problems be written out for her so that she would only have to write in the answers.

Almost overnight her grades went from failing to passing. She even got a couple of As on her first report card.

The psychologist also spoke to the athletic director, who put Sherry on the weight lifting and track teams. Sherry became the school's first holder of a triple record, with state marks in weight lifting, shot put, and discus. Sherry now plans to go to college and become a physical education teacher or coach.

*   *   *

Rebecca seemed to have trouble with everything. She couldn't talk right, she didn't understand most of what was said to her, and as for homework, it seemed to take her forever to do even simple projects.

Other kids often picked on her, and several of her teachers said she should be in a class for emotionally disturbed or special education students. However, her father didn't believe she fell into either category. He sought out specialists to evaluate her and find what kind of help she really needed.

The tests she was given showed that she actually had quite a high IQ, but also numerous learning disorders. One was a *discrimination disorder*. Like Steve, if there were conflicting sounds Rebecca literally could not hear the teacher. Another was a *sequencing disorder* that made a jumble of the order of words, letters, and numbers. Still another was an *expressive disorder*, which made ideas she tried to express—either written or spoken—come out poorly.

Understanding these disorders helped Rebecca overcome them to some degree. Even so, with a gifted younger brother, Rebecca sometimes felt left out. One day, as they were driving to school, Rebecca began singing in harmony with a song on the radio. Her father stared in astonishment. "I didn't know you could do that."

Rebecca was mildly surprised. "Oh, yes, I do it all the time. It's fun."

A few days later she and her brother both tried out for Honors Choir. She made it. He didn't. The choir director told her father, "That young lady has a wonderful voice. She's really musically gifted."

We believe a lot of kids are like Steve, Laura, Sherry, and Rebecca. They should be in gifted and talented programs, or at least have their special abilities recognized, instead of being considered "slow" or problem learners.

Why Steve's problems were not caught earlier no one could exactly say. He had received routine testing of the kind most schools provide. His parents were not professional educators; they simply accepted the school's conclusion that their son was a slow learner, definitely not a scholar.

It happens. In a way perhaps it is understandable, as teachers struggle with overcrowded classrooms, increasing behavior problems (drugs in school, guns in school), massive (sometimes seemingly pointless and certainly endless) paperwork, and (seemingly endless) salary battles and contract hassles.

So it is very possible that you may be gifted without anyone (except perhaps you) having recognized it.

Even if you know it yourself, you may find yourself in a situation like Laura's, with the main focus of her education on her area of least ability and least interest, totally ignoring the area in which she has truly outstanding talent.

We believe this is a problem in many schools: too little individual attention, too much attempt at standardization. Many educators, if they had their way, would turn out a glorious mashed-potato sandwich—a bland, colorless, and characterless parade of kids, all mediocre in math, mediocre in English, mediocre in civics, mediocre in science—instead of one kid brilliant in math but barely passing in English, another brilliant in science but just squeaking by in social sciences or government, a future Pulitzer Prize winner who needs a calculator to do the most elementary arithmetic like balancing her checkbook.

We do understand, to some degree. Teachers tend to consider their subject the most important in the curriculum. The English teacher believes—and correctly—that if you talk like Hillbilly Hank and say "I seen" and "He done" and "I should have went" it is going to hurt you in life. The math teacher knows that if things involving numbers don't come easily to you, you are going to have problems in life. Social science teachers think you need to learn to live in the world community, not like a barbarian, and, again, there's truth in that.

However, they tend to miss the point that a lot of people are very successful in life and have just those failings.

Teachers also tend to specialize in subjects that came easy to them as students. Even though we are learning more about learning disorders all the time, there is still a feeling on the part of most teachers that, "You could learn that if you really *tried*. If you just applied yourself, it would come easy."

Another point teachers often miss is that if you are doing the thing you do best, polishing your best skills to shining excellence, everything else tends to fall in line.

For example, in the books *Yeager* and *The Right Stuff* it is noted that when Chuck Yeager became the first man to do what many felt could never be done—break the sound barrier—some Ivy League type in the nation's capital said, "Keep that damned hillbilly out of Washington!" Some people felt so strongly that a hillbilly, which Yeager certainly was, could not be presented as the nation's newest aviation hero that it was months after the flight before the public was told of the feat. Yet Yeager went on doing what he did best and polishing his leadership abilities, flying expertise, and social skills to the point that he eventually was made a general, something unheard of for a man with only a high school education.

Certainly, if a subject is required and it is not easy for you, you will have to work harder than others in the class. But don't agonize over it, or let anyone make you believe that a lack in one area means you are slow or don't have skills, or even gifts, in another area.

A learning disorder may be your problem, and that should not scare you half to death. A number of learning disorders are labeled *developmental*—a developmental arithmetic disorder or developmental reading or writing disorders. Basically they merely mean that, for some reason, those abilities did not develop at the same rate as your abilities in other areas. It might even be that your giftedness in one area is the focus of your growing brain, and all your ability is concentrated there. Other skills just have to wait their turn.

And there's nothing wrong with that.

There are probably people who are professional level ballerinas as a hobby and who make their living as brain surgeons. And All-American football players who are also Rhodes scholars. But they are very rare. Much more common are people who are good in just a few things, or even in one thing.

Certainly being gifted is not likely to do you a whole lot of good if you don't graduate from high school, and that may mean that some classes are going to be real bears and require all the effort you have. Recognize that as a trade-off, balancing the classes you love and breeze through as a star or even a superstar. Don't let the bummers become the focus of your life and education. You are stuck with them for now, so give them your best shot and keep your eyes on the field in which you know you are good.

The bottom line is that if you don't feel dumb, you probably aren't. Get a professional evaluation if at all possible.

Try to understand yourself and your abilities better. Try to see what is there even if, right now, no one else does.

CHAPTER ◇ 4

Dumb Myths about Being Too Smart

J ohnny is sixteen, and when he graduates from high school next year he will be the first member of his family ever to do that. His family are country people, backwoods people.

"Come on," he says with a wide grin. "Face it. We're hillbillies. Mountain Williams! There's just no other way to put it." The grin fades a little. "My dad's a smart man, but he never went past the eighth grade. And Mom—you couldn't find a better, kinder, harder working person in the world, and she's smart too, common sense smart. But Mom can barely read and write."

Johnny had made straight As from first grade. A second-grade teacher, picking up on his musical ability, talked him into taking piano lessons. Now he plays classical piano—in a part of the world where anything but country and western isn't even considered music. He already has a full scholarship to an Ivy League college.

One day he overheard his Aunt Belle talking to another

relative about him. Aunt Belle, who dropped out of the seventh grade to get married at fourteen, said, "You know, I worry a lot about Johnny. I just don't think Eb and Lizzie is gonna raise that boy. He's too smart. Some people is just too smart to live. The Lord didn't intend it." The other relative nodded solemnly. Both of them really believed it.

Johnny wanted to laugh but also found the conversation unsettling. After all, he came from the same background as these people and had many of the same beliefs. He knew that he wasn't "too smart to live," but it was odd hearing someone say that.

Sounds pretty funny to most of us, doesn't it? Yet these people really believed it. And that is not so funny. Many common beliefs about gifted, smarter-than-average people are equally silly. And about as true.

- **Genius is right next door to insanity.**

We've been hearing that most of our lives, right? A current country and western number has the singer saying he'd rather take his girl to McDonald's than have a gourmet dinner with the butler serving excellent food and fine wine. He wants to stay a common man, because "highbrow people lose their sanity."

When someone extremely intelligent does something a little odd, it usually attracts more attention than it would if an ordinary bloke did it. University professors are often considered "eccentric" for habits or mannerisms that wouldn't even be noticed in shoe salesmen or auto mechanics.

The plain truth is that "Genius is next to insanity" is totally and completely wrong. In fact, the opposite is true. With the single exception of manic-depressive disorder, which is sometimes found in more intelligent people, it is as you go *down* the socioeconomic scale that you are likely to encounter insanity, mental illness, and crippling personality disorders.

• **Most genius-level people can't deal with everyday things.**

Once again, everybody thinks it's funnier when a college professor or a doctor can't remember where he left his umbrella or parked his car than when a plumber or telephone repairman does it. True, smarter people can be a bit more absentminded than the average simply because their minds are busier, more active, not concentrating on everyday details. But as a whole, this myth too is false. The smarter you are, the better your life tends to be all the way around.

• **When you're smarter than average there has to be a trade-off.**

In the cartoon stereotype the class athlete has a single-digit IQ and the class "brain" wears glasses the size of manhole covers and is scrawny, uncoordinated, and always the last to be picked for any game.

For the most part, that isn't true at all. Smarter people are healthier, and they also tend to be more active and athletic than average, even in the teens. The difference becomes more noticeable with the years because the smarter people both stay active and take better care of themselves.

It is the above-average people who play golf, sail, ride horseback, play tennis, jog. The average couch potato, staring at whatever flickers on the tube, also tends to be average or even below average in brainpower.

· **Mentally gifted people are usually doggy-looking.**

A friend of one of the authors might find that amusing. She is a board certified specialist in reconstructive surgery *and* a former Miss Oklahoma.

Once again, although there are exceptions, in general this myth is not true. It seems almost unfair, but gifted people tend to "have it all." Both boys and girls tend to be more physically attractive than the average.

As with health and fitness, the difference becomes more noticeable as these people grow older because they have the intelligence to make the most of what they have and, usually, the money for the best hairstyling, the best makeup, the right clothes, even cosmetic surgery.

In this area girls and women have a definite edge. There are teenagers who are beautiful but not particularly bright, but rare is the beautiful woman of thirty or forty who is mentally as thick as two planks. Usually she has had enough intelligence to protect and improve on what nature gave her.

· **"Geniuses" are more likely to be divorced, have kids that get in trouble, and not be able to get along in the world.**

There are exceptions to almost everything in this life, but on the whole this is a myth and its opposite is true. Gifted people do better across the board and on the whole tend to have better marriages, better relationships with their children (who tend to have fewer problems than average), more friends, and better social lives.

· **"Brains" are bookworms, dull and boring, and they lead dull, boring lives.**

It is interesting that every generation has an insult to describe the "brains" among them. "Bookworm" is fairly old-fashioned. Along with it have been "grind," "dully," and "nerd" (although you can certainly be a nerd without being a brain).

"Dull and boring" is a judgment call and often says more about the person making the call than about what is being judged. For example, one member of a history class may say, "This stuff is really boring," while the student at the next desk may have an alert mind that thinks it absolutely fascinating to learn, for example, why Richard III was cast in the role of villain in the murder of the little princes, or how a fanatic like Hitler set events in motion that led to the horrors of World War II.

The first student simply doesn't have the brains or imagination to see these things. (Perhaps he or she is merely too lazy to make the effort, but we think the first explanation is more likely to be true.) The second student has the intelligence to see that these were real people, these things really happened, and the intellectual curiosity to want to understand how they affected history and by extension our lives today.

The average student with a report to write is likely to trudge to the library, look up a few references, finish the report, and then concentrate on something *really* important like baseball batting averages or NFL team standings.

Let us give you an example. When the teacher assigned a paper on hot air ballooning, Troy, a C to B- "average kid," moaned and complained, checked out a couple of books and skimmed them, wrote the report (it got a C), and promptly forgot about the whole thing. The most important thing in life to him was how his team was doing in the baseball divisional championships and who was likely to make the World Series.

Tim, president of the Honor Society, was in the same class. He read the books and started to write his report, then began to wonder what it was really like to ride a balloon. He called a local businessman who owned one, explaining about his assignment and asking if he might watch the next time the balloon flew. The businessman invited him to do better than that—to go for a flight with him.

In his report Tim included what the books had not mentioned: that they usually flew the balloon at sunrise or sunset because the air was more likely to be calm then, that the ground crew used electric fans to start inflating the balloon with moving air, that it was distinctly odd to feel the little jerk that meant the basket or gondola had left the ground. He described the roar of the butane burners that make the balloon fly. He mentioned that animals on the ground tended to go bonkers when they heard the burners roaring like a demented dragon in the sky. He noted that cows ran and dogs barked, but they didn't look up; only horses looked up to see what in the world was over their heads. The report, need we say, got an A+.

Does Tim sound dull and boring to you? Which guy do you think has the more interesting life? Which do you think other people your age would prefer to have for a friend?

As always, there are exceptions, and some brighter than average people are dull and do lead dull lives; but on the whole this stereotype is wrong. Smarter people are usually more interesting just because they *are* brighter than average. They are more curious about the world around them, more interested in the way it and everything in it works, have livelier imaginations, are more creative.

· **Gifted people have perfect lives.**

Obviously they don't. Being gifted is by no means a guarantee that you'll have an ideal or even a placid and peaceful life. As events of the 1980s and early 1990s showed, some very gifted people landed face down in a whoopsy—people who made millions on junk bonds or this or that kind of fraud and wound up in jail.

· **All gifted people become rich.**

Gifted people do have an edge, but they have no guarantees by any means. Sometimes this notion is part of the resentment that other kids may direct at you. They are sure that, probably before you are thirty, you'll be a millionaire.

You might be, who knows? Some gifted people are. But plenty of them have to struggle in life too. Now and then some fail outright. We imagine there are street people, homeless people, who are gifted. Being gifted won't help you all that much if you don't also have determination and perseverance. Success in life means getting up one more time than you fall, and that takes guts and backbone as well as what's between your ears.

· **Gifted people don't have to work or study hard.**

Some areas come easier to you than to other people, certainly, but you probably know that this myth is not true. You do have to study, you do have to work hard.

*   *   *

Don't buy the dumb myths about being too smart.

It's probably genetic. Men who are brighter than average are more likely to be successful and tend to marry women who are better looking or smarter than average— and vice versa. As a result, if you are in the gifted category and so are your parents, you really are more likely to "have it all."

Don't let anyone put you on a dumb headtrip that makes you doubt that.

CHAPTER 5

Truths about Being Smarter Than Average

We have examined the myths about being gifted and found most of them to be silly and just plain not true. There are a lot of truths about being gifted, however, and they are both in and not in your favor.

- **People expect more of you.**

That is true, and it's not always a plus. Being gifted does not always mean being smart in every area. That can be tough if, for example, you breeze through every class but math. Sometimes it is next to impossible (or maybe just plain *impossible*) to convince your teacher or your parents that you are really having a hard time.

- **People tend to give you more responsibility.**

Lori is fifteen, the oldest of five children. The others range in age from twelve to three. Lori is in the gifted and talented program at school, although none of her siblings are. Their mother has just gone back to work, and increasingly Lori finds herself expected to take over her mother's role at home. She has to pick up her little sister from the neighbor who cares for her and take charge of all the kids until Mom and Dad get home.

"It's not fair," Lori says in a low, unhappy voice thin with stress. "Every single thing they do wrong is all my fault. Like the time the boys were playing ball behind the house and Mark broke a window. I'm the one who got yelled at. And when Jennifer swallowed a jack I was blamed for it. I'm always hearing, 'If you're smart enough to make As in school, you should be smart enough to handle these kids! Why can't we leave you in charge without their getting in trouble?'

"Mom and Dad don't remember that the kids break windows or swallow things when they are in charge. I'm supposed to be smarter than average, so when I'm in charge somehow the kids are supposed to become little angels. I'm smart. I am *not* a miracle worker!"

- **When you talk like the average college junior, adults tend to forget you've still got two more years in high school.**

That is part of Lori's problem; her parents are putting her in a role she is still too young to handle.

It is also a problem for Margo, fifteen, the daughter of a Ph.D. father *and* mother.

"Margo had gotten an unexpected check from her grandmother," her father said, looking sheepish at the memory. "Mom had leased some mineral rights to an oil exploration company for a lot more money than she had expected, and at the windfall she gave each grandchild a check as a gift.

"Margo is saving toward buying a car when she's sixteen. Well, naturally, she was thrilled with the money and went right out and spent a good chunk of it on something I thought was really stupid. It was a jacket, overpriced by three or four times, and with The New Kids on the Block or something equally dumb on the back.

"Anyway, I chewed Margo out for 'wasting her money' and 'being silly and immature' and 'not using better judgment.' Margo was in tears when my wife came home and jumped all over *me*. She said, 'Margo's just fifteen! It's what the other kids are wearing. What do you expect of her, anyway?' That really stopped me. I guess it sounds crazy, but I was used to talking to Margo like an adult. She *is* only fifteen, and I'd been expecting her to display the judgment of a woman twice her age."

- **You tend to expect more of yourself than the average kid does.**

This is true. Generally you realize you have more ability, and you want to stretch it to the limit. Usually you enjoy being better. But it has a downside as well. It is easy to push yourself too hard, to demand absolute perfection— for example, to copy a paper for school five or six times because of some tiny, or even imagined, flaw.

Too often, when this happens, it is because a young person has a distorted view of himself—perhaps feeling valued or loved *only* for his or her brains and ability to make good grades and be academically outstanding.

- **If you do something odd or even really stupid, you never hear the end of it.**

All too true.

Rick is now sixteen. Four years ago, on a dare, he pulled the ancient prank of putting a tack in the teacher's chair. But the teacher didn't sit on it. The hotheaded, mean-spirited principal did, and the class saw a pyrotechnical explosion of a temper notorious throughout the school system. That was four years ago, and the kids—and teachers and his parents—are still bringing it up.

"All right," Rick says, in extreme exasperation, "it was a really stupid thing to do. Don't you think I know that now? It was a stupid kid's trick, and I was a kid at the time! Other kids in school have done things dumber than that. I guess because I'm always on the honor roll it is worse for me to pull a dumb prank than for anyone else. Lay off, will you?"

- **You probably find things funny that a lot of other people, including adults, do not.**

You can be absolutely brilliant and have all the sense of humor of a stuffed owl, but the reverse does not work. A sense of humor starts with at least average intelligence and increases with the IQ. (People of below-average intelligence tend to laugh at things like pulling a chair out from under someone. They also find humor in comedians whose act consists of being foul-mouthed and putting people down.)

Most people laugh at comedy like the Three Stooges— that doesn't take a lot of intelligence. It does take brains to enjoy, for example, the dry British humor of mystery writer Dick Francis, or some of the one-liners from the old Mary Tyler Moore TV show.

Walk through any clinic or university building that has a lot of professors' offices. The cartoons you'll most likely see on display are from "The Far Side." The response of many people to "The Far Side" is, "I don't get it."

So you may often find yourself cracking up at something other people totally miss and wouldn't find funny even if you explained it to them. Which can give you a reputation for being "a little odd" or eccentric or whatever (which you probably find even funnier).

- **You will probably be a leader in your community.**

True. You will probably have greater poise and assurance, especially later in life. You see more sides of an issue than do average people, and you also have the ability to make the right assessment of issues. All this makes other people tend to trust you, look to you to make the best choices, and—by leadership—help them make the best choices.

- **You usually stay in school longer.**

You are more likely to get a bachelor's degree and an advanced degree. Partly that is because you have the ability, of course, but partly it is because you need to be the best you can be in life. You want more out of life than the average Joe—or Josephine.

- **You find less intelligent people boring.**

This can be painfully true.

Laurel, a senior in her school's gifted and talented program, says of her boyfriend Brad, "He's a really smart guy; he wants to be a doctor, and all our teachers tell him to go for it. But his family! I think they must have found him on the doorstep or something. They like for me to go over there a lot, but to tell you the truth they drive me batty. His dad and brothers are baseball freaks—I *hate* baseball! The last time we were over they spent the entire Sunday dinner and most of the afternoon arguing over who pitched in a World Series game back in the '60s. I mean, who *cared*?

"They talk about other people—and not even interesting people. I remember another time when his mom and older sister spent hours talking about his aunt and how she didn't get along with her youngest daughter-in-law. The entire afternoon, rehashing what one said to the other and whose feelings were hurt and who left in a huff. They acted like it was a confrontation between George Bush, Gorbachev, and Saddam Hussein or something. Often when I'm around them I break out in a rash. I think it is from being bored out of my skull and trying not to show it. You can't imagine how stressful that is."

• **You want more time to read, or just think.**

You are rarely bored, especially by your own company. Typically you like to read and spend a fair amount of time at it. You also like to think, and you probably have an active imagination that can take you places and let you experience things far outside the scope of most kids your age. And that's all right. In fact, that's fine. If you are a bit of a loner, there's nothing wrong with that.

In fact, most people who do become wealthy have a strong streak of the loner in them. They are busy with their own plans, and ideas, and thoughts. It's a plus, not a minus.

• **Your interests may bore others.**

As we said earlier, you tend to go much more deeply into a subject than the average person. You want to know what happened, understand why it happened. You are not content with the skim-the-surface attitude of other kids.

Don't worry if they think your interests are boring. You *know* their interests are boring.

- **Others consider you peculiar.**

Unfortunately true. See the next chapter.

- **You are, all in all, going to have a better life than most people.**

Yes. True.
Count your blessings.

CHAPTER ◇ 6

The "Mediocrity Is Better" Prejudice

Dumb old joke: Business owner, "Sorry, son, I don't have anything for you right now."

Young man, "But sir, I know I'd be good for your business. I have a college degree."

"Hmm . . . well, maybe I do have something after all. Okay, you can go to work right now. Start by scrubbing the floor."

"But, sir, I have a college degree . . ."

"All right, all right, I'll show you how to do it."

Dumb old joke: "What does the average college graduate call the average high school dropout ten years after they both leave school?"

"I don't know. What?"

"Boss."

*   *   *

Dennis was thin, wore glasses, was somewhat on the quiet side—the kind of kid you barely notice in most situations. He got along well in school, was well enough liked, never stood out at anything. His grades were average. Then, when he was fourteen, his family moved and when he entered a new school he was tested. His astonished counselor found that he had an IQ of 140. Far above average, actually borderline genius.

When she asked him why, with intelligence like that, his grades were mostly Cs with now and then a B, he had to struggle to put the reason into words.

"When I started school, when I was a little kid, I made real good grades. I *liked* to study and learn new things. But the other kids were always beating up on me, giving me a hard time, calling me a sissy or queer or stuff like that. When I quit making the best grades in class, they stopped. Most kids like me when I don't get anything above the grades I have now."

Terrell's father was an outstanding high school athlete who later was a Little League coach. Terrell's two older brothers are athletes as well, one now in high school and one in college. Terrell's older sister is a basketball and softball star.

Terrell is not as athletic as the rest of the family, although he works hard at it and practices constantly.

When he was thirteen his parents were asked by the school counselor to come in for a conference. The subject: Why doesn't Terrell, who has a very high IQ, make much more than average grades?

"Well, why, son?" his father demanded.

"Well, uh . . ." Terrell gulped, squirmed in his chair, and finally got it out. "I didn't think it was okay. I mean . . . I guess I've heard you say a million times that you'd rather have a son who was a 'regular kid' and could hit a baseball out of the park than," his voice dropped into a wicked and entirely unconscious imitation of his father, "some pinhead junior rocket scientist whose nose is always stuck in a book."

There is in America, and apparently always has been, a definite prejudice against intellectuals, against people considered "too smart."

In the 1950s, when Adlai Stevenson ran against Dwight Eisenhower for President, one of the "charges" frequently made against Stevenson was that he was "too smart," an "intellectual," that he talked over the head of the "common man." For the fairly arduous task of running the country, it seems logical to us that you would want the smartest man or woman you could find, but no—most people "liked Ike" and elected him for two terms.

If a politician is also a Rhodes scholar, that is not played up. The image he tries to project is "smart, maybe, but still a common man."

Think of all the so-called teen movies you have seen, from the 1950s "beach movies" to the present. Sometimes there was a character identified as a "brain." He was usually skinny, bespectacled, somewhat nerdy. Although he occasionally saved the day for everyone, he was not the hero and he didn't get the girl. Even the Smurfs show this attitude. Brainy Smurf, horn-rimmed glasses and all, is also the dingbat who gets the other Smurfs into trouble with his lack of common sense.

Many kids who are smarter than average find themselves, like Dennis, the target of bullies, accused of being a sissy, given a bad time.

This seems to be pretty exclusively an American characteristic. In most other countries the intellectual stars are given honors and prestige—and opportunity. Here we are more likely to give honors, prestige—and money—to some athlete who is barely able to hold his own in a conversation with a rock.

By no means are we saying that all athletes are dumb. Quite the contrary. "Dumb jock" is another myth that needs to be done away with. We are just saying that the single-digit-IQ athlete who earns millions is definitely a fact of life.

Perhaps the prejudice came about because so many people came to America to escape persecution and hardship. To reach the point where you could persecute and oppress someone else, you usually had to have enough brains to acquire that much power. Perhaps nobody wanted to look like a former (or future) oppressor, so the goal became to be "just a regular guy." Just one of the faceless crowd.

Interestingly, the prejudice diminishes as you go up the educational and socioeconomic scale. Kids, particularly little boys, who are smarter than average in grade school can find themselves the object of all sorts of negative attention from other kids. That, however, diminishes as they get into junior high and high school and disappears by college.

The reverse is true for gifted girls. It is slightly more okay for little girls to be smarter; they don't get quite so much negative feedback. But as they enter junior high and then high school the vibes begin to turn negative for them.

In high school being a "brain" becomes increasingly more acceptable—the brainy senior gets a little more respect than the brainy freshman. (Other people tend to like to study with you!) In college, "brains" come into their own. They become the elite on campus.

The ordinary, clock-punching blue-collar worker often distrusts and dislikes "brains," listens to songs on the radio of the glory of being a "common man," and may actively discourage his kid from high scholastic achievement. The bank president, the doctor, the rocket scientist has no such prejudice. Typically, he or she is aware of being smarter than average, and no kid of his or hers is going to get away with average grades.

But there are more blue-collar workers than bank presidents, and at your age this prejudice can be rough— one of the real negatives about being gifted. You are still on the receiving end of the "Mediocrity is better" message.

Everyone is urged to go for "the American dream"—to be rich and successful. Yet on every side we are bombarded with messages saying that that really isn't the way you want to be.

For example, consider the people on soap operas such as "Dynasty" or "Dallas." These are very wealthy people who make (or at least supposedly spend) millions, live golden glitzy lives—and are miserable. They pull fantastic deals and rake in the money, but when it comes to running their own lives and their relationships with others, they don't just shoot themselves in the foot, so to speak, they do it with an Uzi. The underlying message is, "Although these people are rich and successful, they have miserable lives and relationships that are always in turmoil. Be content with being a middle-class, middle-of-the-road, plain vanilla American."

Teachers often single out the brightest kids in the class and pick on them endlessly. Girls may prefer to go out with the football star rather than the guy with the 4.0 grade point average. Kids may want to study with you but then may make nasty remarks behind your back.

How do you cope?

First, realize what is behind a lot of it. You are making them look bad by comparison. The biggest factor in the resentment of other kids, most of the time, is just plain jealousy, and jealousy is a lousy emotion whether you're feeling it or receiving it. Telling people they're acting like jerks because they are jealous can get you anything from denial to a punch in the nose—even though that is exactly what they are doing.

Family attitudes may be behind some of the hostility. We have heard of uneducated redneck types telling their kids, "You don't take nothin' off nobody. Somebody acts like they're better'n you, give 'em a punch in the mouth." (Actually, everybody is better than someone like that, including some of our relatives who haven't made it down out of the trees yet.)

You may do more than just make other people look bad. Being around someone for whom study and learning come easy may make them sharply aware of their own limitations and shortcomings. They feel inferior, and they don't like it a bit.

The best way to cope with jealousy, we believe, is first to study your own behavior and be sure you aren't doing anything to make the situation worse (see the next chapter), and then basically ignore it.

If you are the target of serious bullying, of course, talk to a teacher or a counselor about it. But don't be tempted to drop into the swamp of mediocrity just because a bunch of bozos are pressuring you to do it because it would make them feel better! You have been given a better than average brain or skill or talent, and your life, in most cases, is going to be better, happier, and more successful than theirs. That may not be a lot of comfort now, but believe us, shutting off your brainpower to make them feel better is not the answer.

Why be average when you can shine, be an academic superstar?

We hope the mediocrity attitude is changing to some degree. A number of schools have begun to honor their academic as well as athletic stars with special recognition programs in assemblies, privileged parking places, credit cards good in local stores, bumper stickers for parents saying, "My child is an honor student at Yukon Middle School," and other perks like that.

We think that's great! The prejudice is still there and probably will be for a long time, but we're taking steps in the right direction.

No, we haven't forgotten that you have to live with the problem now. Keep reading.

CHAPTER 7

If Other Kids
Don't Like You . . .

Warren at fifteen was undoubtedly one of the smartest kids in school, if not the smartest ever to attend. He was also one of the most disliked. He was regularly challenged to fight, ambushed in dark places and punched, poked fun at, and put down. It never seemed to bother him until one afternoon he turned pale and sat down on a bench, bending over and saying he felt sick. Teasing began by the other boys, until suddenly Warren vomited almost pure blood.

Rushed to the hospital by ambulance, he was found to have a perforated duodenal ulcer that required surgery. Later, talking with a counselor, he confided tearfully that he hated feeling hated, that he had begun to think about suicide.

Warren's background was unusual. His father, a university professor, wrote history textbooks and was considerably more at home in ancient and medieval times than in the present. (When they had a sensational murder in the neighborhood, one of his teachers asked Warren what his father thought about it. Warren snorted and said, "He's in the middle of a book on ancient Rome right now. The last violent death he's really aware of is Julius Caesar's.")

Warren's mother was an artist and college art professor who painted in a fey, otherworldly style pictures that featured unicorns, fairies, elves, and other mythical creatures. She too seemed most of the time to be out of touch with reality. Warren had been a late, unexpected (and—he always believed—not particularly wanted) baby. He had been raised in the house where his parents had lived for years, among neighbors who were for the most part elderly. He rarely saw any other children.

When Warren was four the family moved to Europe while his father did research. Until the boy was ten, he was taught at home by his mother. He attended public school for the first time in the fifth grade, and he had next to no experience in getting along with other kids. He knew nothing about current music, current styles, and the latest interests of kids his age. They had not had a TV set in Europe and had one in America only because his grandmother had given him a set for Christmas.

Children can be and usually are very cruel to one another, especially to one who doesn't "fit in," and they turned on Warren like small scavenging animals. He had never experienced anything like this, and he was terribly hurt and upset. But his parents refused to take his problems seriously, coming up with clichés like, "Sticks and stones can break your bones but words will never hurt you!" (Which, by the way, is 1,000 percent wrong.)

Warren was an outsider and didn't know how to be anything else. He didn't know how to fit into the world of his classmates. But he knew he was smarter than most, or any, of them. His brain became his weapon. He would fight back with that. He wielded it like a Ninja sword. He not only made straight As, he lorded it over kids who didn't do as well, made nasty remarks when someone got an answer wrong, and rubbed it in over a poor test score or grade.

His doctor turned Warren over to a counselor, and slowly and hesitantly he began to learn some social skills. It was very difficult; he had maintained his pose of sneering superiority so long that it was second nature to him. But gradually he learned. He made a friend, the first young friend in his life, and then another and another. He offered to tutor other kids and found he had a flair for it. He began to enjoy their successes. By the time he reached his senior year he was not the most popular kid in school but was generally well enough liked. He would go on to become a Big Man on Campus in college.

Tony's parents divorced when he was ten years old. His father, a career military man, was out of the United States most of the time. His mother was a morose, bitter woman whose complexion and outlook were as gray as the clouds of smoke from the four packs of cigarettes she went through every day. She rarely had time for Tony and his younger sister.

Tony was far brighter than average, but all it seemed to have gotten him was trouble in school and bullying and abuse from other kids. Then, one day when Tony was fourteen, a kid on the bus started talking about a street gang he belonged to. It gave Tony an odd twinge inside—the kid talked as if it were something special, belonging to a gang. Tony had never had a feeling of belonging anywhere or to anyone or anything. He asked the kid how you got into a gang.

At first the kid, knowing Tony's reputation as a nerd, was reluctant to take Tony with him, but finally he gave in. Some of the members were talking about shoplifting in neighborhood convenience stores. Tony had thought about shoplifting, although he had never done it. Now, hesitantly, he voiced some ideas he had—possibilities the other kids had never thought of.

The gang members were electrified. Hey, yeah, man, that'd work! Boy, the neat stuff they could walk out with . . . thanks, pal, we think you'll do all right hangin' with us.

That was two years ago. Today Tony is in serious trouble with the law, charged with being both involved in and the brains behind a liquor store robbery in which a clerk was shot and seriously wounded. The district attorney is trying to get him certified to be tried as an adult. One of his arguments is that Tony's IQ is genius level; he of all people should know the difference between right and wrong.

Tony's father has raised Cain and his mother screams and yells at him nonstop. He is asking to go back to jail.

Nobody understands that it was *because* Tony was smarter than average that he got into the gang in the first place. Rejected by other kids because he was so much brighter than they were, and not having the social skills to overcome that "handicap," Tony found a place where he could belong.

Gangs will accept anybody willing to go along with their activities. And more than belonging, in the gang Tony found acceptance and appreciation *because* he was so smart. Smart enough to figure out new and foolproof ways of shoplifting, getting, using, and selling drugs, committing robberies, stealing cars.

Gary was never more than an average student, but he was a great athlete. He was captain of the basketball team, all-county halfback in football, and had a .310 batting average.

Gary also had a problem: He didn't know how to just have fun. Both of his parents were alcoholics, and Gary spent a major amount of his time taking care of them or his younger brothers.

Other guys at school considered Gary strange. They said things like, "He's in great shape, but he just doesn't get it." They teased him by telling jokes that he didn't understand. Girls seldom dated Gary because he didn't know how to talk to girls. In fact, despite his athletic abilities, Gary was very lonely and very isolated. He desperately wanted what most kids took for granted—a friend.

Finally Gary attempted suicide. The school was stunned. No one in the school or the community could believe that such a talented teenager could be so miserable that he didn't want to live.

If you see anything of yourself in Warren, Tony, or Gary, what do you do? How do you cope?

First, ask yourself some questions. Do you lord it over kids who are not as bright as you are? Do you, like Warren, brandish your superior intelligence, twist the knife when someone else makes a mistake or gets a lower grade than you? It may make you feel good at the moment, but in the long run you will feel as isolated as a leper dumped on a deserted island.

Superiority can be good armor. Like armor, it can protect you from being hurt. But also like armor, it keeps anyone from getting close to you. It keeps away the warmth and the friendship we all very much need.

Do you ever act impatient or irritated when other kids don't catch on as quickly as you do? Again, the little boost to your ego is temporary, but the cumulative effects can be disastrous.

Social skills—the ability to get on with other people and be liked and accepted by your peers—are tough to learn if you didn't grow up absorbing them automatically. As a general rule, kids have roughly the same degree of social skills as their parents. If that is not a thought that makes you happy, don't despair, because there is a lot you can do about it.

First, hit the library. There are tons of books on the subject, many of them excellent. (See the Rosen book *Coping through Friendship*). If your school library doesn't have many or any that seem to help, go to the public library.

Watch people who are popular with others. And *don't* fall into the trap of thinking that you have to be gorgeous, or a hunk, or a football star, or rich, or whatever to be popular. If you stop, look, and analyze, you'll probably find that some of the most popular kids don't fit into any of those categories, and yet everyone likes them.

Don't just watch, *study* what they do and how they do it. Learn to analyze behavior. This girl that everyone likes—is it because she's a great listener, because she really *hears* what people say to her? Is that guy so well liked because he has a good sense of humor, one that laughs with people, not at them?

One of the great secrets of being liked is a simple one: People like people who listen, really listen, and who keep private matters private and don't spread them around. Sound too simple to work? Try it. We assure you it isn't.

Study people who get on your nerves, and why. You can learn a lot that way too, once you begin to analyze.

Do *you* like the jerk who's in love with the sound of his own voice and can't stand not to be the center of attention? Or the girl who can't open her mouth without slamming someone else? Or the braggart who seems to go through life with his horn stuck—no matter what you or anyone else has done, he or she has done it more often, better, more excitingly?

The person who, if you say, "It's a pretty day outside," will give you an argument. Or who says, "The TV this morning said there was a 20 percent chance of rain. I'll bet it rains just about in time for the football game. I don't care because football is a stupid game for Neanderthals who haven't got anything better to do. Anyway, we're probably going to lose, so why bother to go or have a game at all?" (This is known as giving every cloud a pitch-black lining, and there are few more irritating people in the world than those who do it.)

The person who is so self-absorbed that no matter what is going on he or she doesn't respond or ever really listen?

You don't like them—neither do most other people.

Practice behaviors that feel right to you. If you are on the quiet side, you are likely to fail and look pretty foolish if you try to turn yourself into a rah-rah, bounce-off-the-wall cheerleader type. Try out a joke or a bit of conversation on one person who seems friendly or at least as if he or she won't reject you. Ask questions. And *listen* to the answers. (We can't stress that enough. The one thing that will go a long way to help you be liked is to learn to be a good audience. Everyone sometimes needs an audience.)

Let your abilities be a plus for other kids. Volunteer, in a quiet, low-key way, to help tutor someone who is having a problem. Whatever you do, don't allow yourself to be (or even to feel, because it is sure to show) patronizing, superior, or snotty about the fact that the subject is easy for you and not for the student you are trying to help. Remember that he or she has an ability you don't have right now—the ability to get along well, to be liked by other people, the ability to have friends.

If your school has a program for students to tutor other students, you might volunteer. If your gift is athletics, help other students learn how to bat, how to make a three-point play, pass a football, or whatever.

Join a club that involves something that really interests you. Study other kids in the group and their behavior. Volunteer, and don't get on your high horse if you are handed the jobs that the Navy calls "scut work"—sweeping the gym floor before or after a dance, tacking up miles of crepe paper. Do them well and cheerfully, and if you have time, volunteer to help other people stuck with scut work. Sure, if you have good ideas contribute them, but don't get huffy if no one pays much attention.

Learn to laugh along with other people even if you don't find something particularly funny (unless someone is being hurt by it, of course.) Your sense of humor will probably be different from a lot of others'. You are more likely to enjoy "Bloom County" or "Calvin and Hobbes" than "Marmaduke" or "Garfield." Enjoy the laugh itself, not the reason that is provoking it in other people.

Having people not like you hurts, really hurts. And it can be dangerous, even lethal. Isolation can trigger depression that in young people often ends in a suicide attempt, or even suicide.

Every now and then someone gets in trouble whom no one would suspect of it—like the son of a doctor arrested for housebreaking or the lawyer's daughter for dealing drugs. Most often the key to such behavior is what this chapter has covered—more than average ability in certain areas but not enough social skills to fit in, have friends, be "just a regular kid."

CHAPTER 8

Teacher Troubles

One of the reasons being gifted has its own special burdens is that too often you are accused of being the "teacher's pet." What's worse, a good part of the time you not only are *not* the teacher's pet, but the teacher seems to have it actively in for you!

Yes, it's true. The author who is a former teacher has seen it happen (and hopes she hasn't been guilty of it!).

Why in the world would a teacher be after the scalp of the brightest kid in class? For a number of reasons.

One, we think, is that teachers are only slightly less prone than the general public to fall into the "Mediocrity is better" trap.

While the niece of one of the authors was in grade school, the class had a special visitor who asked questions of the kids, including who was President of the United States and who was governor of the state?

Margie was the only one who knew the answer to both questions. As she recalled it, "The teacher acted really miffed about it, and she went to great lengths to explain to the visitor that it was only because I was a lawyer's daughter and a newspaperman's granddaughter that I knew about things like that—rather as if I were a kid who knew more about the facts of life than I should have at that age! She acted kind of ratty to me for several days after that. I never did understand it."

Friends who are the parents of a gifted five-year-old said his kindergarten teacher was highly irked when, as she was introducing the children to "Mr. A, Miss M, Mr. J," their son was reading on a third-grade level. She said it "wasn't fair to the others."

According to students in another school, the teachers' kids were privileged characters. As one boy put it, "The teachers' kids are supposed to be the smartest. If you do anything to show up one of their kids, boy, your name is mud with all the other teachers."

For the most part, extra-bright kids are the favorites of most teachers, and who can blame them? Those are the kids who sop up knowledge like a sponge, whose performance in class makes the teachers look good. Naturally they are favorites.

But by no means is even that picture totally rosy. If being "teacher's pet" gets too much negative reaction from other kids, the "pet" simply stops excelling, stops trying, stops turning in outstanding work or doing other things to shine. Or he or she may become a behavior problem— anything to mark him or her as "just a regular kid."

Bright kids also can and often do drive teachers batty because they think up and ask about things that even most teachers have never considered.

Larry, in the third grade at the time, asked his teacher quite seriously, "When birds hop around on the ground, are they looking for worms or are they listening for worms? They put their head on one side so that their ear is down toward the ground—it seems like maybe they are trying to hear the sounds a worm might make. Or maybe their eyes are so far around on the sides of their head that they have to point an eye to the ground to see what's down there?"

The teacher, who had never given a thought to how birds hunt worms, stared at Larry as if a Martian had materialized in her classroom. When he persisted with the question—because he really wanted to know—she became angry. Was this kid trying to put something over on her? Make fun of her? Make her look stupid? She had never heard such a silly question. Furthermore, she hadn't the foggiest idea of the answer. Brusquely she told Larry to sit down and be quiet. The rest of the class wound up giggling at Larry.

(For the record, scientists tell us that birds put their heads on one side because—as Larry had guessed—their eyes are on the sides and are less mobile than the human eye. That's the only way birds can look straight down.)

Gifted kids drive teachers bonkers for other reasons. They are more easily bored and antsy in class. They can breeze through an assignment in half the time it takes everyone else, which leaves them with nothing to do. To a teacher it is frustrating. As one history teacher put it, "I have three really smart kids in my class. They finish everything long before everyone else, then have time to get squirmy and antsy and bored.

"Their minds go off onto something totally unrelated to what the class is working on. When they finish an assignment, they start to think about other things, or read something not related to history. They've tuned me out. They aren't thinking about America's early colonial period, they're mentally putting the finishing touches on a space rocket, or designing cars they think would be really neat. Mentally, they are not in my classroom.

"I give them extra work sometimes, but they throw a fit and say it isn't fair. It is and it isn't, if you know what I mean. It's a real problem sometimes. But our school doesn't have a gifted and talented program, and I don't see any solution any time soon."

To be honest, some teachers just can't stand the idea that that mouthy high school version of Bart Simpson in the front row is smarter than he or she is. Not as knowledgeable at this point, of course, but smarter. When that feeling surfaces you can have a real case of being "picked on" by a teacher. We have heard of a case or two in which a student has been hounded into dropping out of school by this type of teacher. It's rare, thank goodness, but it happens.

How do you cope with either extreme—being "teacher's pet" when that status is causing you problems, or having a teacher who seemingly wants to display your head on the wall over the mantel?

Transferring out of the class is something to consider; if it's possible, it might be the easiest solution.

But first, in either situation, collect some evidence. Make notes of times, dates, and things that happen. It is possible, in looking back through your notes, that you'll find you are a little too sensitive, or overreacted to something that in retrospect was not such a big deal. That is not to say that you never have a legitimate gripe. A lot of the time you most certainly do!

At any rate, when you sit down to hash things out with the teacher, you'll have something more solid and convincing than a nebulous, "I feel you're always on my case and picking on me. It makes me hate to come to class."

Whether "teacher's pet" or "teacher's hate," we suggest a frank talk with the teacher.

Explain that it can be hard to be the "pet." In effect you are telling the teacher to stop being so nice to you and favoring you above the other kids, and that can be very hard to do. But explain that it is making life difficult for you, and you would prefer being just "one of the guys." That may not work, and it may make the teacher angry. Sometimes accusing a teacher of favoritism will really transform you from "pet" to "picked on" in one easy step.

It can be just as dangerous (probably more dangerous) to accuse a teacher of picking on you. Most indignantly deny that they would do such a thing. (That is another reason having a careful written record can help.) Some teachers honestly are not aware of their antagonistic attitude. If you can demonstrate it, you may get a little more equitable treatment.

If none of this works, in either case, it's time to move up the ladder of authority. See a school counselor or the principal and explain your problem. And take along your written record.

If that doesn't help, or you get brushed off with something like, "Oh, don't be silly," it may be time to bring Mom or Dad into the act.

Getting on the bad side of a teacher—especially when it is basically because you are smarter than the rest of the class—can be a yearlong problem. But look at it this way—it's only for one school year, which can seem like an eternity but certainly isn't.

Solve the problem between you and the teacher if you can, of course, but if you can't, just stay cool and bide your time. In a few months you'll be out of there and the demon will be just a bad memory.

CHAPTER 9

Family Roles

H unter's parents are both medical doctors, although his mother works only part time. His older brother is a pre-med student. His sister, a senior in high school, has a 4.0 grade point average. Hunter's is 3.8. His younger brother and sister are about as smart as the rest of the family. They are a warm, loving, close family and share many activities and interests.

One morning in school Hunter looked tired and had dark circles under his eyes. When a teacher commented on it, he shrugged it off with, "I was up until almost two this morning, working on a paper for English. I just couldn't seem to get it right."

Now the teacher is worried about Hunter, worried that he may be under too much pressure at home, that his parents may be driving him with an expectation of perfection.

Jake has been a "brain" from his first day at school. His parents are awfully proud of him and let him know it. His dad frequently says, "You're the hope of the family. I know you'll do better in life than I ever did." Jake fervently hopes so—his father is a blue-collar worker in the auto industry, with little hope of advancement and frequent layoffs. The family's existence is sometimes very much hand-to-mouth.

Jake would like to go out for sports, but when he does it cuts into his study time and he finds it harder to make top grades. He dreams of playing basketball but thinks it would be letting his folks down.

He feels tremendous pressure, and under it a lot of anger and rebellion that lately have been giving him stomachaches.

Tonya's father is a biostatistician with a master's degree. He is an elder in a church that believes children and women should be seen but not heard. He shrugs off women's lib as "a lot of hogwash" and turns purple at the mention of abortion rights. Tonya's mother is a meek woman who has never been "anything but a housewife." Tonya can never remember hearing her argue with her father about anything important.

Tonya's older brother is the "family star," as she puts it. An outstanding football player, he also did well in high school. In his first year in college he is maintaining his 3.2 average despite playing football there as well. Tonya's parents are very proud of him and talk a lot about his athletic ability and his grades as well.

Tonya's grades have always been higher than her brother's. She has rarely made less than an A, or a 100. But, when her parents go into the "brag about the kids" routine, that is never mentioned.

Li Chiu Yeh was born in America and considers herself American, although her parents are refugees from Southeast Asia. Li Chiu is sixteen. When she was thirteen her father died and her mother's mother, an iron-fisted tyrant, came to live with them. Grandmother rules the house; not even Li Chiu's mother opposes her.

Li Chiu and her older sister and two younger brothers must come straight home from school and study until bedtime. They are not permitted to bring friends home or to visit friends after school or on weekends. Neither Li Chiu nor her sister Kwan are permitted to date, even though Kwan is twenty-two. Kwan is an honor-roll senior at a nearby university but is not permitted to live on campus. She still lives at home and abides by the same rules as her younger siblings.

They cannot listen to rock music, watch TV, or wear clothes Grandmother does not approve. They cannot take part in extracurricular activities at school, even though they all want to. They cannot even object to any of this—they are told often and angrily that failure to respect one's elders is the worst crime a child can commit. Li Chiu is lonely and isolated. Kids like her at school, but she has no real friends.

Li Chiu has become more and more depressed. She discovered recently that, in spite of Grandmother, Kwan is secretly buying liquor and drinking on her way to and from school. Li Chiu is terrified that Kwan is close to suicide. She herself thinks about it a lot. "Why not?" Kwan said angrily one day when they were talking about it. "Could death be much worse than this life?"

Juan's family are racetrack people, working as grooms, "hot walkers" who walk a horse to cool it down after exercise.

His father dropped out of school in the sixth grade, got a job as an exercise jockey, then later rode in races. But he lost his jockey's license and served a term in prison for trying to fix a race. Now the family live on the backside of tracks, follow the racing season from track to track, much like migrant farm workers. Sometimes Juan and his sister Caretta go to a half dozen schools in one school year.

Juan's father speaks minimal English and doesn't read or write it at all. Suggestions that he go to school to improve his English meet with explosions of anger. Actually, just about everything meets with explosions of anger. Juan's dad is a morose, sullen man, resentful and envious of everything anyone else has.

Juan's mother is the daughter of a college professor. Frequent angry clashes with her parents during her teen years led her to elope with a jockey she had known only a couple of months. She has had no communication with her family since. Juan has never seen his grandparents. His mother is a silent, withdrawn woman who is the target of much of the father's anger. Sometimes their battles are frighteningly violent.

The family travel from track to track in an old bus. They are far below the poverty line. If it were not for other people on the backside and the racetrack chaplains who help out, Juan and Caretta would never have decent clothes to wear to school.

In spite of this unpromising background, Juan is very smart. He knows that brains and education are a way out of a life that is miserable most of the time. He would probably make straight As if he had any cooperation at home. But instead of cooperation he gets active opposition. The sight of Juan or Caretta studying sends their father into fits of anger. "What you tryin' to do?" he bellows, "be better'n me? What kinda system is it tries to make a son feel like he's better'n his old man? Takin' care of horses is good enough for me and it's gonna be good enough for you, too, you hear? You HEAR? I catch you at them books again, I'm gonna whale ya', you unnerstan'?"

Only intervention by track authorities and the chaplains have kept the children in school, kept the father from physically abusing them. Even so, he constantly does things like throw away school books or assignments Juan and Caretta have slaved over for hours.

When Juan ran across the passage in *Huckleberry Finn* where Huck's drunken father throws a fit because Huck can now read and write and the old man can't, Juan told Caretta, "You've got to read that. Brother, talk about empathy!"

Tony's dad is a small-time hood who has—to Tony's knowledge—taken part in four bank robberies and drawn two terms in prison. His mother's specialty is shoplifting, although she has also driven the getaway car in a couple of convenience store holdups. Through luck and technicalities, although she has been arrested several times she has never been convicted. Their friends are similar people—police characters whose world is made up of dope deals, burglary rings, mad dashes for Mexico in the middle of the night, and who's doing time and who needs bail.

All of them make fun of authority figures, especially the police, judges, and most lawyers. Tony is often in trouble in school. His parents find that funny and a plus, proof that he is like them. They never scold him even for the worst things he does.

In spite of this background, Tony is bright, very gifted intellectually. He can get a locked car door open faster than most people could open it with a key, and he can lift a wallet from a man's pocket or a woman's purse without their suspecting anything has happened. He even invented one of two of his parents' "cons"—confidence tricks.

One of Tony's teachers has seen his real ability and his potential. She is also aware of his background and fears it is only a matter of time before Tony finds himself in serious trouble with the police. She is doing everything she can to direct him into academic excellence and a real future.

Tony sees the idle life his parents and their friends lead, with no need to punch a time clock or pay attention to a boss. He understands the kick of being able to thumb one's nose at authority.

He also understands the fear they all feel at just seeing a cop drive past their house. In spite of the crime, he also understands that basically the family has next to nothing. Their standard of living is at the poverty level. He wonders how the freedom of not having to please a boss could possibly equal the stress of knowing that any minute you could be arrested and thrown in jail. He remembers as a small boy visiting his father in prison and having nightmares for years afterward about being locked in a cage.

He hates always being in trouble at school and not being liked very much. He would like to dump his background, change his life, change the way he sees himself heading. But—his parents love him and are proud of him the way he is. When he thinks of turning his back on their values and establishing his own, making his own life, he feels disloyal and guilty.

*   *   *

All of the above are examples of family roles that being gifted can cause you to play. Such roles can be a heavy burden or just very unpleasant.

The teacher's worry about Hunter was not justified. Everyone in the family was brighter than average. It was simply expected that Hunter would do well. He felt that expectation, but not as pressure. It was the way he was raised, the way the family was. Staying up until 2 a.m. now and then wasn't going to kill him, or even do more than make him yawn a bit the next day. And certainly he didn't feel compelled to do it every night. Because the family was warm, loving, and close, Hunter did not rebel against being expected to excel in most things.

Jake's role was a little different—and more difficult. Jake was exceptional, and his family was very much aware of it. Jake was cast in the role of "family hero." He was the one who would give the family economic stability, security, perhaps in the future make enough money to take care of his parents. He was the hope of the family in a life that was mediocre and at times uncertain.

Tony was in a position that forced him to be a "people pleaser"—trying to live up to the role his teacher wanted for him as well as the role expected by his criminal family. Between the two forces he was pulled like a wishbone; no one seemed to care what the real Tony wanted to be and how he wanted his life to go.

Because in Tonya's family women were not valued but were treated as second-class citizens, Tonya was ignored or made fun of for her academic excellence. Often the response of girls and young women to such treatment is to think, "Why bother? It doesn't matter anyway," and to quit trying to excel in school or to follow their own dreams.

Many young people of oriental background find themselves in Li Chiu's shoes. The tradition of learning and excellence and respect for one's elders is very strong in those of such ancestry, but it can be taken to extremes that are not healthy—in fact are dangerous, as in this case. Li Chiu's grandmother is overreacting to a change in life-style. She had lived most of her life in Southeast Asia, coming to the United States in her 60s, when adjustment and change are difficult. Now she lives surrounded by an alien culture that she dislikes and distrusts. In trying to hold on to the culture of her own people, she refuses even to consider that she may be doing harm. She will not admit that her grandchildren are Americans. She is forcing them to live as aliens in an alien land.

Juan was in the most difficult position of all. His role might well be characterized as the "family lightning rod," or perhaps the "family threat." His father used Juan's academic excellence to vent his anger at the world. He also felt threatened by a son smarter than himself. He was afraid his son's brain would topple his macho "king of the mountain" view of himself.

A healthy family in which you have a healthy role is made up of "balcony people," wrote Joyce Longdroff in her book *Balcony People*. Balcony people sit in the balcony or stand in the wings and cheer you on.

Unhealthy families, like most of those described here, are made up of "basement people." They lie around at the lowest level of life and try to pull you down to it. They hate the idea of anyone's winning because that makes it all the more obvious that they are losers.

What do you do if your family role is not a healthy one but is causing you problems in life?

First, recognize that your family and how they feel are not your responsibility.

You owe them some degree of loyalty, yes.

You do not owe them a human sacrifice—yourself. You

do not owe them your life, to be lived according to what they want if that is not what you want. Unfortunately, "basement people" parents are usually very good at pulling "guilt" strings to make you feel that you owe them everything.

Dealing with a family role that pulls you down is very difficult. Don't try to cope on your own; any success you have will probably be limited. Get outside help. Talk to a teacher or a counselor. That can be very difficult, because you probably do love and feel loyalty to your parents. It can be hard to tell an outsider that you think your folks are trying to ruin your life. Most of the time they are not doing it consciously. Most of the time they have no idea of the effect of their actions or expectations.

If your school doesn't offer such help, try outside resources. Many large churches have youth ministers, trained to help young people with problems. Be a bit cautious, though; get a recommendation, perhaps from a teacher, if you can. And if the person you talk to seems more interested in converting you to his or her way of thinking about religion, or offers simplistic advice such as "Just pray and put everything in God's hands," keep on looking for help somewhere else. (Certainly we believe in God and think prayer helps, but that alone is rarely the answer.)

In some states certain facilities have been designated as "safe places" (for example, fire stations.) This is mainly for kids and teens in serious trouble, but it means that someone there has been trained to deal with, or find someone to deal with, kids with problems like those we have discussed.

You may be put in touch with someone in the juvenile court system. That may sound scary, but it needn't be.

Such people have resources for kids with problems before those problems push you to the point of breaking the law. They would always rather prevent crime then try to "cure" people who have committed it.

In Juan's and Caretta's case, arrangements might be made for them to stay after school and do their homework there, so they won't arouse their father's anger and push him to destroy what they have worked on. There is also the possibility of their asking to be put in a foster home, away from an abusive father and a bad home situation. That is a big and frightening step and not one most young people would consider easily, but it is a possibility.

Some states permit emancipation of teens, under which a court can grant semi-independence before the legal age of adulthood. That means that the teen can live alone and not be held accountable or obligated to parents. Usually it is done to get young people out of an abusive home situation. Occasionally they can take younger siblings with them and act as a temporary guardian.

Usually, the teen is closely supervised by a social worker.

Emancipation is not an ideal situation, but sometimes it is better then trying to remain in the home. A threat of such action in the case of Li Chiu might have made the grandmother relax her demands to avoid losing face as a person doing bad things to her grandchildren.

Another powerful weapon in the case of someone like Juan's father is the threat of being arrested and held for a sanity hearing. The threat of winding up in a mental hospital often stops such people when a restraining order won't even slow them down.

What if your problems at home are not serious enough to warrant such drastic action. We still say, talk to someone.

Get outside advice and objective help. You have a lot going for you. Don't let family members mess things up for you, even if they are acting out of misguided love.

CHAPTER ◇ 10

Sibling Rivalry

Becky is a pretty, popular, easygoing teenager who has considerable musical ability and is an excellent dancer. She makes "good enough" grades but comes nowhere near the academic peak of her younger brother, Brian. Brian is gifted in almost every field he has ever tried.

Becky wishes she had some of Brian's academic gifts, but she is not jealous or envious of her brother's abilities and accomplishments. She admires them and would like very much for him to be closer, to be a real friend.

Brian holds his sister at arm's length. He considers her a complete airhead, much inferior to himself. He rebuffs her efforts to be friends and share things and tells himself it's a good thing somebody in the family has some brains.

If Brian would get off his high horse and take a more realistic look at the situation, he would see that he could learn more from Becky than she could learn from him.

She could teach him to dance, and some of the social graces he lacks. She could probably help him learn to make friends—an art at which he has little skill or practice. Actually, Becky has more to offer in the relationship than

Brian does, but using his academic superiority as the only scale, he does not see that and probably wouldn't admit it if he did.

Meg is the oldest in her family, the only gifted one of four children. Since both parents work, Meg has done a lot to help raise and care for the other kids.

Even though the two boys are highly competitive about most things, they don't resent the fact that Meg makes better grades without having to work as hard as they do. Somehow it seems fitting that the oldest in the family has an edge. She has more responsibilities, but more privileges, too.

There is no sibling rivalry here, or no more than you would find in most healthy families.

Amanda is fourteen, gifted, beautiful, a talented musician. She has an older brother, Brent, and a younger one, Mel. The boys have average looks and average brains—and a burning jealousy of their sister, who seems to have it all. So they gang up on Amanda.

Amanda is the target of what she wearily calls a "hate campaign." Her brothers put dead rats in her dresser drawers, leave her standing in the rain when she is supposed to ride home from school with them, "forget" to give her telephone messages, insult her friends. More than once the animosity between them has come to kicking, hair-pulling, and slugging. Amanda has had bruises and black eyes from the fighting.

Their parents, when they hear, or hear of, such problems, just say, "Oh, I wish you kids would stop that." They never discipline the boys. Now and then one parent or the other says to Amanda, "Don't be such a magnolia blossom." (If you touch or brush against a magnolia blossom it withers and turns brown.) "Don't go around with your feelings out on stems just waiting to get hurt. Ignore them."

The parents are blind to the fact that Amanda is becoming more and more depressed, more and more troubled by the situation at home. Her grades and her participation in school events, even musical events, are slipping. Lately she has begun to think about running away.

Kent and Stan were another example of jealousy. Kent was ahead of the average baby in learning to walk and talk. But at age three he fell, hit his head, and was unconscious for several hours. Apparently Kent suffered some brain damage; since then he has been on the slow side in learning. Not retarded, just slower than his younger brother. He made average grades but had to study harder for them.

But Kent was a good-looking, cheerful, outgoing youngster whom everyone liked. And he was a superior athlete, doing almost anything in sports easily and well. He said he wanted someday to be a coach.

Stan, by contrast, was small, thin, klutzy, with none of Kent's "people-attracting" personality. Through grade school, from thoughtless teachers and other adults he heard, "You are Kent Alt's brother? Boy, I never would have guessed it. Are you going out for sports, too? Think you'll be as good as he is?" Stan was sure he never could be.

Stan began to take his frustration and anger out on his brother. He picked on him constantly, called him

"Football-head," "Single-digit IQ," or "BD," standing for "Brain-damaged" or "Brain-dead."

He never did this around their parents, who had no idea how bad the problem was. And because Kent was bigger and stronger, if he went after Stan physically he came off as a bully.

Most of all Stan picked on him in the area of grades and learning ability. Whenever Kent made less than an A or had a problem in school, Stan hammered it home—"I could teach the *dog* to do these problems. Boy, I guess this is proof a human can't be too stupid to live." The effect was to further shatter Kent's already frail confidence in himself and his ability.

Although Kent won an athletic scholarship to the university he wanted to attend, after high school graduation he stunned teachers and his parents by going into the armed forces. "I'm through kidding myself," he said. "Even taking easy courses there's no way I could get through college. This is the best thing for me."

He was deployed to Saudi Arabia and was one of the first to die in the Gulf War.

Stan was shattered, devastated, eaten alive by guilt. "I did it," he said, over and over. "I killed him as surely as if I'd pulled the trigger. To make myself feel better, I nagged and pulled him down. I wasn't half the person he was, brains or no brains."

Stan wound up in an adolescent psychiatric ward. With counseling, he has made some headway in coping with the tragedy, but he says, "I'll never really get over it. I'll carry this with me the rest of my life."

Having a gifted sibling is sometimes no fun at all. Your parents may be smart enough not to put you down, but if they don't you can bet *someone* will—"So you're Tom's brother (or sister). Do you make the honor roll every time, too?" Painful pause. "You *don't*? Uh . . . well . . . . . ." There's not much one can say after that. The nongifted sibling feels like an inferior dolt.

Teachers do it all the time. Relatives can be great at it. "Family friends" do it. Most of them don't think of the harm they are doing to your brother or sister. Sometimes even parents do it. And parents too often fail to act when someone else is about to commit this classic blunder. If the nongifted sibling is hurt, many parents brush it off with, "Oh, she didn't mean anything by that. Don't be so thin-skinned!"

Often the resentment your brothers or sisters feel becomes directed at you. You become Miss Perfect, or Mister Perfect, often the target of hostility by the nongifted. And that's painful. You miss so much in life not being close to brothers and sisters. They can be your best friends, a ready-made support group when things go wrong in the world, your quickest and best allies because they understand you and the way you think and react. Maybe in the area of book-learning or talent you hold a slight edge, but you share the same blood and genes and basically you're part of that collection of people we call "family."

As with Meg, if there is only one gifted child in a family, things seem to go more smoothly if it is the oldest. Oldest children are usually expected to take a leadership role. Younger children may occasionally resent that, but they usually accept it with less trauma and tribal upheaval.

Playing superior, as Brian did, looking down on Becky, he lost out on a lot of things they could have shared that would have made his life better and happier. He isolated himself right in his own family, and isolation is something most of us don't need in this world.

If a gap opens between you and your siblings, try mending that gap yourself. When you see your siblings as people with abilities of their own, you will probably find a lot they can teach you.

Kent could have taught Stan a lot about sports, perhaps enough so that Stan could make a team. Kent could coach, and he loved to do it. But Stan, in his ivory tower of academic superiority, wouldn't even consider it. They both lost out.

One way to start to break down walls is to ask a brother or sister for a favor: Would you help me with this? Teach me to do that? Be grateful if he or she will. Admire his or her ability and make it genuine admiration. This is your brother, remember? He knows you pretty well, and phony he'll read in about three seconds.

Learn to appreciate the person. Find things you can share and things you can do together. Learn to talk to him or her. Find out what interests your brother or sister. You may learn a lot yourself.

If unfair comparisons are made without your parents or others realizing the damage they are doing, talk to them about it. Tell them that you are being made to feel like the family outcast. Too much building you up just makes your siblings want to tear you down.

If your parents won't try to ease the situation, talk to someone at school, a teacher or counselor. Perhaps they can talk to your parents about it. We believe most parents will try to help. They may make unfair comparisons thoughtlessly, without realizing the harm they are causing. Once you point it out, we think most of them will try for better relations among family members.

Try to get close to your brothers and sisters if you possibly can. They should be your best friends, closest allies, buddies you know will be there for you all your lives.

But if you absolutely hit a brick wall, don't break your neck trying, and for heaven's sake don't feel guilty about it. Simply get on with your life and fill it with other friends.

Surprisingly, giving up trying to improve relationships with siblings may be what it takes to make them better. While you were trying to become better friends, a sibling's refusal to meet you halfway gave him or her the "power" hand. When you no longer care, or try, to get along better, suddenly that power base is gone. You may become better friends after all.

CHAPTER 11

Special Problems
of Gifted Girls

A dam, talking to God: "Tell me, God, why you made women in the first place?"

God: "So you'd like them."

Adam: "Oh. Well, why did you make women so pretty and soft and warm?"

God: "So you'd like them."

Adam: "Why did you make women smell so good?"

God: "So you'd like them."

Adam: "Well, okay, God, but tell me this. Why did you make women so *stupid*?"

God: "So they'd like you."

Julie and Simon met just before her junior and his senior year in high school, when Julie's father was transferred to town by his company. It was "like" at first sight. They began dating, and both began to think maybe they were in love. Simon told his friends he didn't ever want to date another girl. Julie told girlfriends she hoped she and Simon would be together when they were old and gray.

Love bloomed all through the summer. Then school started again and the hot romance began to cool. Simon became critical of everything about Julie. He picked on her clothes, the way she wore her hair, her friends, activities she was involved in.

Poor Julie was bewildered. She hadn't made any radical change in what she had been doing or wearing all along, and yet nothing about her seemed to please Simon any more. He stood her up on dates; and finally, after saying he had to be out of town, he walked into Julie's best friend's birthday party—with another girl. Julie was crushed, getting only faint satisfaction from the fact that her brother took Simon outside and flattened his nose for treating her like that. She couldn't understand why Simon had so totally changed.

Truthfully, neither could Simon. All he could say was, "Everything she did just got on my nerves more and more all the time. I don't understand it either."

Their problem was simple, really. Simple, and yet not simple at all. Simon was an average B−, C+ student, although a talented athlete. Julie was a straight A student, in the gifted and talented program, the National Honor Society, and recognized as one of the brightest kids in school. Her superior mind made Simon feel inadequate, threatened. It rattled his macho. During the summer he had appreciated Julie's intelligence. He was never bored around her as he had been with other girls. But in school he felt it showed him up, made him look less than superior to his girlfriend.

Like many men and boys, Simon felt he had to have a girlfriend who was "inferior" to him in every way—

younger, shorter, and "dumber." His ugly treatment of Julie was simply because at school she was a constant reminder that he was not, after all, "superior."

About children, as we have said elsewhere, there is a kind of unspoken agreement: Boys are supposed to be "tough and dumb," and little girls are supposed to be smart. Little girls are more often admonished to look after little brothers than the other way around. Parents seem to think they are too smart to do some of the things little boys jump into without a second thought.

But at about junior high level, things often start to change. Boys start to realize that their future is closer than they had thought and in their own hands, and they begin to get their act together and put more effort into study.

But this is also when boy-girl attraction, if not actual dating, begins. Girls start thinking about the future too. Traditionally, they start thinking about one day getting married. More thought goes into what boys like. Too many boys are like Simon—attracted to girls who make them look and feel smarter by comparison. They are not mature enough to realize that it's a compliment to be liked by a girl who is more intelligent than average, that it takes something special in a guy to interest and hold such a girl.

Unfortunately, this kind of nonsense does not end with junior high school. A recent tabloid paper had a headline on the cover, "Looking for Love, Ladies? Inside—What Men Really Want." The headline on the story inside: "Men Still Like 'Em Dumb."

That is changing, but slowly. Everywhere now, on TV, in the movies, in books, we are beginning to find examples of bright, achieving women who are feminine and loved and have successful careers as well as good relationships with men. The wife in the old TV series "Hart to Hart" is a perfect example. She was beautiful, feminine, very bright, with a successful and interesting career as a magazine writer. She never took a back seat to her "self-made millionaire" husband. Unlike a zillion "heroines" of old cowboy movies, she didn't stand cowering against a wall with her knuckles pressed to her mouth while three bad guys beat up the hero. Jennifer Hart was likely to wade into the battle swinging a skillet if someone was threatening her man.

In the smash hit "Aliens" there was even a woman warrior without a love interest in the story.

But those are the exceptions. The stereotypes are still everywhere. The prejudice against women who are anything but decorative has been around for hundreds of years. Don't expect it to vanish in just a few.

It is unfortunate but true that women in most societies are not valued for their intelligence. True, in most beauty pageants "the interview" has become a little more important than in the past, and it is less likely that the girl with the one-syllable answers and the single-digit IQ will be named Miss Anything. Still, the emphasis is mostly on the superficial.

According to the male half of this writing team, very bright girls often turn boys off without intending to because they come across as critical or condemning, or as flaunting their own abilities.

An example might go like this. Vince was giving an oral report on watching the beginning of the Gulf War when his career military father was stationed in Saudi Arabia, and what his thoughts had been at that terrible time. He described what he had felt on hearing about the Stealth bombers hitting Baghdad.

Sally, who is gifted as well as very pretty, was identifying very much with all of this—her father was career military too. (Vince would have liked to ask her out, but he hadn't had the nerve.) At this point she put up a hand and said, "They didn't use Stealth bombers, Vince. Those were Stealth fighters. They were certainly bombing, but they were fighter airplanes."

Ears reddening, Vince corrected himself and went on with his report. Sally was still very much wrapped up in what he was saying. In her mind she had only corrected a minor error. She liked Vince a lot. It never occurred to her that he would mind that small correction

But he did. Vince took it personally. Sally's interruption over something trivial had spoiled the effect he was trying to create, the image he had of himself as a storyteller trying to make his audience understand something that had been very important in his life. He felt pinned down, as if all Sally saw and heard were trivial details. As if all that mattered to her was being right.

As they left the classroom he made a nasty remark under his breath to Sally, who was taken aback and bewildered. She had been about to tell him how much she had enjoyed his report and how she identified with what he had felt. Now she stood staring after him, wondering what in the world had rattled his cage? She was never likely to know. Boys in general are not good at feedback. Vince might nurse his grudge for months, but it would never occur to him to tell Sally why he felt the way he did.

Boys—and men—take a lot of things personally in a way that would never occur to most girls and women. If a girl asks a boy out, or to a party she is having, and he says he has out-of-town relatives visiting and can't get away, most girls shrug and take the statement at face value. It's no skin off their ego.

But turn the situation around and if the girl says she has

relatives visiting and can't get away, the boy's reaction is likely to be, "Yeah, *sure* she does! She just doesn't want to go out with me. She probably thinks I'm a wimp or a geek or a big zero. She probably noticed that one zit in front of my left ear." And so on and so on.

The chest-thumping macho exterior some guys put up is an attempt to counter this inner response. Frequently the nasty and cruel things guys say to girls or about them are in response to what the guy has seen as a put-down, when it was never intended that way. Students of human behavior are just beginning to understand the very real and sometimes very large differences in the way males and females think and communicate.

Many people—and not just boys—see smart women as less feminine than their more average counterparts. Perhaps there's something to that, at least as far as superficial appearances go. The girl who puts extra effort into schoolwork, or who would rather read than spend two hours giving herself a manicure, or who thinks inner substance should matter more than superficial style may not be willing to give up most of her evening to do her hair and iron something special to wear the next day.

Of course, these outward trappings have nothing to do with how feminine you really are, but they are what people see and how they tend to judge you.

Some people undoubtedly are still letting their judgment be swayed by images from the women's movement of the 1960s. The women who led the fight for some sort of equality knew they would be discounted if they marched and protested in heels, frilly dresses, salon hairdos, jewelry, and makeup—for the simple reason that they had been discounted for years when they tried to look "feminine" while working for better treatment and equal pay for equal work.

The message to the "feminine" woman was, "Run along home, honey, and don't worry your pretty little head about this. We men will keep running the world as we always have."

So some of the women's libbers adopted an almost masculine, even butch, uniform—shapeless and sexless clothes, straight and often unkempt hair, no makeup, in a few cases combat boots.

Men got the message they were sending—"We don't need you!"—and some of them still equate that message with women who are achievers, brains, accomplished, even when the message is not fair or correct.

So watch how you act and react to situations like Sally's. A far better course would have been for Sally, if she felt compelled to mention the error, to catch Vince as they were leaving, express her admiration for his report, then add, "Oh, by the way, it was probably just a slip of the tongue, but . . ."

Most gifted females at some time in their lives go through the experience of trying to "gear down" in a relationship with a boy or man who is not as bright as they are. It simply doesn't work, not for any length of time. Not without taking a terrible toll on you.

Katie met Ben in their senior year in high school. Ben was an athlete, a good-looking kid with a great personality but average brains. Katie was in the gifted and talented program and among the brightest kids there. But she fell like the proverbial ton of bricks for Ben.

They dated that year and Katie—dazzled—found herself constantly having to rein in her own razor-sharp mind to keep pace with Ben's slower and less challenging (and interesting) brain. They watched a lot of TV, although

Katie found most of it very boring. She had always read rather than watch TV. "I read everything I could get my hands on. But Ben said reading bored him, and it bugged him that I always had my 'nose in a book,' so I basically stopped reading."

They watched a lot of sports on TV. Ben loved sports. He could talk for hours about them, which Katie found about as fascinating as watching paint dry. But for Ben's sake she pretended an interest.

Her own ambitions—to be a writer and to get a master's degree and teach writing in college—she rarely mentioned. Ben thought they were silly and unrealistic.

Ben and Katie went to the same college, still dating. Ben, with Katie's help, managed to scrape through. They married in their junior year. Katie admitted to herself that she was the more capable of the two, the real brains of the couple, but she adored Ben and that was all that counted. It would be all right.

Only it wasn't. More and more Katie came to realize that, in gearing her own mind down to keep pace with Ben, she was cheating herself. She was sacrificing what she wanted to do in life to flatter Ben's ego. She couldn't go for her master's degree because he didn't have one and he would have taken it as an insult if she tried.

If she wrote the book she wanted to write, which knowledgeable friends were urging her to write, it would shatter the facade. The difference in her husband's ability and hers would jump out and hit, not just them, but everyone, right in the face. She doubted if Ben could handle it.

She owed it to herself to write that book. She owed it to her husband to keep the unspoken pact she had made with him when she married him—to be the keeper of the facade of their marriage, the life they had always led and the relationship they had always had, allowing him to preserve the illusion that he was the stronger, smarter, more responsible one of the two.

Katie began to feel pulled apart. She developed migraine headaches, then an ulcer. In trying to keep life as it always had been for her husband, she later said, "I became 'Momma' to him. I had to make sure nobody, least of all he, saw the real differences in us. I had to protect him from the truth, from the fact that my brain could run circles around his. I had to be sure he didn't see that he wasn't the 'lord and master' of the household. You can't imagine what a strain, a constant stress, it became.

"I had once loved him very much, but that love wore out under the . . . well . . . the *burden* of it all. From love I went to resentment and then to actual dislike, and I felt very guilty because of all those emotions that were basically not his fault, but mine. Our separation and divorce were pretty bitter. Each of us felt cheated by the other, and I guess in a lot of ways we really were."

If he's a real doll you'll probably be tempted to try, as Katie tried, to gear down. It works only for a little while, and it may not be worth the strain even for that little while.

Seriously, curl up with a good book until you find a guy who is more your equal or genuinely doesn't care that he isn't and is proud of you for your brains and ability. (But even that doesn't always work, because you get bored with his limitations.)

There are plenty of such guys out there, although you may not find one until you are out of high school. Some high school boys can be awfully shallow—he'd rather pass up asking you out because his friends might think he's dating a girl as smart as he is, or smarter.

Fortunately, this attitude of having to be superior usually changes in college. People who are "brains"—girls as well as boys—come into their own in college. In fact, in college most guys find the Miss Airhead date an embarrassment.

Maybe that is not much consolation now if you are sitting home alone on Saturday nights, but believe us, you'll appreciate it a few years down the road.

And come to think of it, don't you dare sit at home alone *now*. So you don't have a date. Go to a party with a girlfriend, or alone. *Give* a party. Volunteer for a club activity. Help with a project in your church or synagogue. Be a candy-striper in a hospital. Volunteer at a museum. There are a thousand and one things you can do to make life more interesting—and to improve your chances of meeting neat guys.

Work at being happy. Abraham Lincoln once said, "Most people are about as happy as they make up their minds to be," and there's a tremendous amount of truth in that.

Happy people radiate a warmth that draws others to them the way a fire draws people on a freezing day. In fact, many boys and men say that warmth of personality attracted them to the women in their lives even more strongly than sheer physical beauty. If she radiates that warmth, he feels he'll be accepted, warts, faults, and all.

A woman with warmth of personality makes a man feel confident.

Be feminine. Put a little extra effort into the external trappings. Superficial they may be, but often they do matter and can help your image.

Watch how you relate to people in general and other kids your age in particular. Ask for feedback. Sally could have insisted that Vince tell her why he was upset with her. Ask your brother for some constructive criticism. If he gives it, take it and use it—don't either blow up at him or curl up like a wounded armadillo.

Remember that boys take things (almost everything, really) personally and feel rejected very easily. Probably the greater his macho act, the more true that is. Try to see things from his point of view.

Never try to gear your mind down to his in a relationship. It makes for endless misery and frequently breakups.

Some men like 'em dumb, but plenty of men—more all the time—are realizing that the dumb ones don't wear well. In the long run, Miss Airhead is a thundering bore. Those are the men for you. They're out there, we promise. And when you find one like that, you can make all your life a lovely adventure.

CHAPTER 12

Making It in Your Field

"**N**othing in the world can take the place of persistence.

Talent will not; nothing is more common than unsuccessful men of talent.

Genius will not; unrewarded genius is almost proverbial.

Education will not; the world is filled with educated derelicts.

Persistence and determination alone are omnipotent."

—Calvin Coolidge

If you are among those classified as talented, it is easy to see your talent as both a blessing and a curse. You know you have the right stuff to be the next Tom Clancy, Kevin Costner, Meryl Streep, Tom Cruise, Reba McIntyre, Bruce Springsteen, Madonna, Vanilla Ice, Garth Brooks, or whoever.

You also know that for every person who makes it big as a

writer, singer, songwriter, or actor, there are thousands of people who don't.

How do you give yourself every advantage?

First, learn everything you can about your field. If you are a budding artist, take lessons. If you want to be a writer, read everything you can about how to write, how to get published. It is a common misconception (which the talented themselves often hold) that you are born with talent and that is all you need.

Talk to any successful person in your field and you'll learn how silly that notion is. You can *always* learn, always hone and polish and improve your skill.

Join a club of people who do what you want to do. Most communities of any size have writers' clubs, artists' groups, actors' organizations. These can be fun and supportive, and they often lead to opportunities to meet people who can give a genuine boost to your career.

One word of warning, however. We don't know how it is in other such organizations, but in writers' clubs there is always a contingent of people who are "going to" be published. They get together and read each other's stories and tell each other how wonderful they are. That way they get pats on the back without having to risk the rejection slips that go with actually sending something off to a magazine or book publisher.

We think the second-best trait you can have, if you also have talent, is a thick skin. So you get rejected. So what? You have to let it roll right off and try again. Send the manuscript somewhere else. Start another story. Keep *going*.

A friend of one of the authors, a widely published writer, says of her work, "I have no ego tied up in it, and I think that's at least as valuable to me as being able to write. While I'm working on something, it feels like a chunk of my soul. But the minute it goes in the mail, it's like a typing job I hand to my boss. It irritates me if it is rejected, but I certainly don't take it personally.

"But I have known writers, or more likely would-be writers, who get one rejection slip and are crushed. A lot of them never try again. And you can't do that. You just can't do that. Success in a field that requires talent is like success in almost anything else. Success means you got up one more time than you fell down."

Try to get help from people knowledgeable in your area. Get them to criticize your work, but *only* if they have some background for doing it. A university professor who teaches writing might be willing to look over your manuscript and give you some pointers. A college-level art teacher might have some advice that your high school teacher doesn't. Ask, and be generous with your thanks if these people do help you.

Write to people in your field. Ask for advice, ideas, suggestions. (Be lavish with praise when you write, of course. Most artists and writers respond to it.)

Writers are driven crazy by aspirants who say, "Won't you just look at a couple of chapters and tell me what you think?" One of the authors heard Tony Hillerman respond with, "I'd really rather not. It's *your* book. If I tried to change anything it would be to the way I'd have written it, not the way you did. Just make it the best you can now and send it in."

Our advice follows Hillerman's: Get advice any time you can, but the most important thing is to make the story or book the best it can be that day and send it in.

We say "that day" because so many would-be writers or artists want to wait, thinking that somewhere down the line they'll be better. *Don't!* As the commercial says, just do it. Tomorrow you might be a better writer, but the way you get to be a better writer tomorrow is by writing something today.

Never miss a chance to showcase your work or yourself. Write and submit things. Paint and enter every show you can, particularly juried shows, which have awards and prizes. Prestige comes to artists who win them. If you can't star in local productions, take bit parts or even volunteer to work backstage. You'll learn and gain from it.

Study the work of people who are successful and whom you admire. How did they do what they did? Know what you are studying, of course. Madonna has an undistinguished voice and the vocal range of a penny whistle. She has become a megastar on showmanship, not singing.

Making it in any field requiring talent usually requires an even greater degree of persistence. Determination. Going after it one hundred percent.

Set goals in your life. We're for writing them out and putting them where you can see them every day. What do you want to have accomplished by the end of this year? By the end of this month? Today?

Maybe persistence and determination alone are not all-powerful, but you are unlikely to go much of anyplace without them.

CHAPTER 13

"Something to Fall Back On"

You are the one people call talented—you're a singer, a dancer, a writer, an artist, an actor. You'd love nothing more than to be a great success in that field.

You also know that the odds are enormously against you. When planning for college, or a career, or even the rest of high school, should you pursue that dream, or should you be practical and choose another career so you'll have "something to fall back on"?

We think you can do better than either extreme.

Visit the college or university you are interested in and talk to people in the field you want. Get their advice. You will probably find some options you didn't know existed. If you want to be the kind of artist who has devotees waiting eagerly for his or her next painting, you don't have to shoot for that as your only goal. In the fine arts school of any university they'll teach you that you can work as a commercial artist (designing ads, perhaps, or painting sets for TV or movies) until the Metropolitan Museum of Art comes looking for something of yours.

A lot of people who want to write become reporters first. Plenty of actors made TV commercials before they ever saw their names up there, as they say, in lights.

College will help you in more ways than just teaching you how to improve your talent and showing you fields where you may not have thought of using it.

Colleges try hard to place their graduates, and they have connections you couldn't begin to find. Just being a student at that particular college may open doors. If one drama department graduate is now on Broadway and doing well, the casting director will look more favorably on another one. (You.)

The publishing world is full of graduates of the University of Oklahoma professional writing program. Apply for a publishing job in New York with that OU degree and you've already got points in your favor; the editor interviewing you is likely to be an OU grad too and know of others doing well.

If you are pursuing a goal that only a few reach, however, we do think it's a sound idea to give yourself something to fall back on. If you want to major in drama, why not minor in education? Then you can teach drama too. Major in professional writing, minor in journalism. Tony Hillerman was working for the Associated Press when his first novel came out. Fred Stone painted sets for movies and TV shows before he began the paintings of horses, mostly Thoroughbred racehorses, that have fans lined up waiting to buy prints.

We do think you should set goals for yourself. In your first few years out of college (or high school, but we can't too strongly recommend college), if you don't have a family and financial responsibilities, you can probably put all your eggs in one basket and go for your dream. Live in a broom closet and on canned soup and try to break into the Broadway stage. Live in an attic on boiled potatoes and try to write the Great American Novel.

But set a goal. By such and such a date you want to have accomplished such and such. If you haven't done so, maybe it's time to start getting a career established. You need not give up on your dream. Just convert it to a hobby, an avocation, a part-time thing. (Tom Clancy was working as an insurance salesman when he electrified the world with *The Hunt for Red October*.)

Talent can feel like a curse. Sometimes it seems to have a life of its own and drive you relentlessly. You paint a picture, or write a book, to get free of the thing! The sister of one of the authors, describing a movie she was directing, said, "It's like being fourteen months pregnant," and we can't think of a more apt description.

Do give yourself something to fall back on. It's not a cop-out, or selling out. Hang on to your dream, keep pursuing it with determination. But don't wreck your life because of it.

CHAPTER 14

If Your School Doesn't Have a Gifted Program

Gifted and talented programs in schools are designed to give students with special abilities a head start in putting that ability to the most productive and profitable use. Unfortunately, not every school has such a program and, as mentioned elsewhere, we believe that not every gifted and talented person is included in the category.

What do you do if that's your situation?

We'll start with four basic pieces of advice:

- Go to the library.
- Go to the library.
- Do special projects in your field of interest.
- Go to the library.

We're only partly kidding. As we have said, the more you find out about your area of special ability, the better your preparations and choices are likely to be, and the more likely you are to find what is available to you.

The school library is not the only one. The public library should also have a lot of information. Read everything you can find about your own abilities and how they can be used, about the career field that interests you and what you want to do with your life.

Once you are knowledgeable about your abilities and where you want to use them, you might find it possible to work in that field—in an internship, for example.

Margo planned to major in journalism and mass communications in college—her fondest dream was of herself as a TV news anchor. She wrote for the school newspaper and read up on the media business in general. When she learned that a national network was coming to town to televise a college football game live, Margo was first on the telephone, telling the network she wanted to work for them while they were there. And she got the job.

To some people it would not have been a particularly impressive job. Wearing a bright orange vest, she spent the game trailing along behind the cameraman at the edge of the field, pulling the cables of his camera so that no one got tangled up in them. It wasn't exactly fame or glory, and the pay was nothing to brag about, but nevertheless she could put the job on her résumé. She was the only kid in her high school who had ever worked for a national TV network. In fact, she beat a lot of college kids to the punch on that one.

So it won't exactly open doors in New York. It was fun, it earned money, and it certainly isn't going to hurt her. Plus, she saw the game from a vantage point only a few other people had. She wouldn't have known that national TV crews hired local people to do things like pull cable if she hadn't read as much as possible about the field she wanted to enter.

This summer she plans to apply to all the TV and radio stations in town for temporary or part-time work. So she just answers the telephone or delivers mail. She'll be learning. Bright and talented, Margo is giving herself an edge in what she wants to do in life.

Consider the possibilities of special schooling. Admittedly, this is a hard choice—to think of leaving your friends and familiar territory now just to give yourself an advantage in the dim future. But it's something to consider.

Many large school systems have special schools for gifted and talented youngsters. New York and Los Angeles both have schools for the performing arts, where young people who dance in Broadway musicals or work on TV series also attend high school. Oklahoma City has a School of Math and Science for kids with special abilities in those fields.

You might not want to consider leaving your school to attend a special school, but perhaps you could take a few extra classes there each week. Look into it. It can offer real opportunities.

Consider local colleges as well. Community colleges are usually open to you even if you haven't graduated from high school yet. It is common for gifted and talented kids to graduate from high school with a whole string of college credits already earned. Even major universities frequently make exceptions and admit high school students for one or two classes in the area of their special ability. Most colleges have no hard and fast rules in this regard; each case is decided on its own merits. It is quite possible to enter college as a freshmen with a year or more of college credits already chalked up.

Consider asking your teachers for special projects. Gifted and talented kids find that the ability to learn new things, to work their minds, compensates for the extra work.

A teacher of a math genius who was studying college math and physics at age thirteen said, "Lenny's like a raging bull. You just get out of his way."

Lenny said, "It's fun to do this stuff. There are no ill effects as long as people don't call me a nerd."

So be your own coach, your own driving force, to learn and to do and to be and achieve as much as is possible for you.

The bottom line of all this is that it's as much fun, and feels as good, to stretch the muscles of your mind as the muscles of your body.

For most gifted young people, once you get started in your field you are like Lenny—there's no stopping you.

CHAPTER 15

How Can You Tell

if You're Gifted?

t is easy to assume that a person with a gift or talent would know it. Unfortunately, although some kids know almost from birth that they are special, others do not. In fact, they may never discover it.

• **Could you have a gift you haven't discovered?**

Ross had never thought of himself as special. He made average grades and had ambivalent feelings toward school. He came from a fairly ordinary family. He dated occasionally. He tried out for various sports, without success, and felt sure he wasn't a jock. On Saturdays and most afternoons he worked for his father in their grocery store. He was a hard worker, and his father often said Ross could move and carry twice the load he himself or the other man who worked there could.

When his father fell on ice and broke his leg, Ross had to double his hours in the store, sometimes working until midnight or later stocking the shelves and helping to unload merchandise.

Ross noticed that he was getting stronger, that his muscles were beginning to show. He realized that the girls were noticing too, and he liked that. But he still never thought of himself as gifted.

Then one day Ross went to a fitness center with a friend. Although the friend had been working out for years, Ross could bench press and military press more weight than he. While they were at it, the high school coach came in. He watched Ross for a few minutes, then started him on some routine weight lifts. He asked Ross to come and see him the next school day.

Soon Ross was in training for a regional weight lifting competition, which he won easily. He then went into training for a state competition. The coach began talking about national, international, even Olympic events.

According to the coach, "That kid is the best thing to come down the pike since Arnold Schwarzenegger."

Jenna was a tomboy who loved to ride the horses on her grandparents' farm. She would jump on a horse bareback and go tearing across the pasture, riding like an Indian, jumping streams and fallen logs.

One day a neighbor who had been a famous equestrian saw Jenna riding. She stopped on the road to watch and then drove up to the grandparents' house. "If someone is willing to put some money, time, and effort into training that girl," she told Jenna's parents and grandmother, "I think she'll be world class before she's through."

At first it seemed too farfetched an idea for any of the adults. Then a few weeks later they happened to see a broadcast of the annual Rolex jumper competition held in

Lexington, Kentucky. That was enough to persuade them to pay for regular riding instruction.

Jenna was eleven then. Today, at eighteen, she is preparing to compete for the team that will represent the United States at the next Olympics.

- **People may always put you down about your ability. Or your family may not value that skill.**

From the time she could hold a pencil Celia doodled and drew pictures. She was always attracted to art and often said that when she entered a room the first thing she noticed was what was on the walls. Celia's farm parents, she also often said, made the painting "American Gothic" (the farmer and his wife and a pitchfork) look like a pair of revelers on a romp through a Paris nightspot. They were good people, but very conservative and totally without imagination. To them, anything "different" from the way life had always been was threatening; "sameness" was highly valued.

Celia once commented that, where she was concerned, her parents acted like a hen with one duckling. (The hen makes no distinction between the chicks and the duckling until the day the latter takes to the water, which chickens don't do. Then you have on your hands a case of hen hysteria!)

Certainly Celia's parents had no appreciation of her ability. The mere mention of artists and models suggested to them vague naughtiness—nude posing, wild studio parties, the usual stereotypes about people who make their living in a creative field. To them, the idea that people would pay *good money* for pictures was as remote as Alpha Centauri.

They chided Celia for "wasting her time" drawing, and it

certainly never occurred to them to spend money on books or drawing and painting materials. When Celia bought artist supplies out of her allowance, they were angry with her for wasting her money and sometimes grounded her for it.

It was not until she took an art class in high school, began to emerge as a star of the class, and then won a state competition that anyone—including Celia herself—began to see that she had real ability and could possibly make a good living—and, who knows, even achieve fame and fortune—as an artist.

- **Perhaps everyone in your family is to some degree gifted, and you don't see yourself as out of the ordinary.**

Leta's father was a newspaper editor, her mother a published poet. Her older brother had been editor of the high school paper and was now editor of the paper at college, where he was majoring in journalism. Leta wanted to be a writer, but in English composition she regularly made Bs and Cs. Discussing a college major, she was surprised when the school counselor suggested professional writing.

"But Mr. Hansen," she said in bewilderment, "I don't have any talent in that field at all. It's what I'd most like to do, but I don't think I'm good enough to make a living at it."

"You're more than good enough. You're better than your brother."

"But . . ."

"I know how most of the English teachers in this school grade, and I strongly disagree with it on English composition. They usually grade strictly for correct usage—nouns where they ought to be, verbs where they ought to be, no dangling participles and all that.

"You have to know good English to be a writer. You have to know how to do it right before you can get away with doing it wrong. But good writing, particularly good fiction, has to be the way people really talk. You have to grab the reader. Look at the best seller list—those books slaughter the rigid rules of English on every page, but they're what people *read*."

"But I'm not that good . . ."

"In your family you are not particularly outstanding, that's probably true. But don't you see, where other people are concerned all your family are outstanding."

Leta followed his advice and is currently on the honor roll in a professional writing program at a university.

(For the record, if you want to make a living as a writer, we recommend that you find a school with a professional writing program. Creative writing, in many schools, means writing for self-expression and self-fulfillment, and occasionally to impress others. A professional writing program teaches you to write for *money*.)

So you may feel you have more than average ability, or a talent, but you aren't sure. How do you find out?

Basically, we believe that the more things you try, the more likely you are to find something in which you have above average ability. Experiment. Try new things. How do you know you can't be a good chess player, writer, singer, athlete, artist, or whatever if you have never given it a try?

Who would have thought one could be an outstanding success in life beginning with lifting boxes of groceries or riding a horse bareback?

Below is a quiz that might help you discover whether you're gifted or not. Answer yes or no.

1. Do you sometimes think you know more about a particular subject than do other kids your age?
2. Do you listen to adults discussing a topic and find yourself feeling sure they have missed something important?
3. Do you solve problems in ways that make people say, "I'd never in a million years have thought of that"?
4. Do you often find yourself bored with things that amuse your friends?
5. Is there anything you do better than your friends?
6. Are you often surprised that other people have trouble with something you find easy?
7. Do you watch someone struggling with a project and instantly know that he is going about it all wrong?
8. Do you find a lot of school lectures boring—and obvious?
9. Do you sometimes irritate adults or experts in a field by asking questions that stump them?
10. Do you find yourself saying things like, "They were both right," or "It's all a matter of perspective"?
11. Do you "see through" things other people say?
12. Do you find yourself asking, "I wonder what he/she really wants?"
13. Do you laugh at jokes that others don't understand?
14. Do you like to sit quietly and think, and feel unhappy if you don't have time for your own thoughts?
15. Do you enjoy your own company and rarely feel bored when alone?
16. Do you like being around bright, witty people?

17. Do you find yourself wanting to stay after class to discuss things with a teacher?
18. Do you ever question your minister's or rabbi's sermons?
19. Do you sometimes think that you could have done it better than whoever did it?
20. Do you ever develop your own theories about an issue?
21. Do you create new things (a new recipe, a new hairdo, your own clothes, a design for a carpentry project)?
22. Do you ever apply something you learned in one field to an entirely different field?
23. Do you like to try new, different, or exciting things?
24. Do you like to read the newspapers? Do you watch TV news shows like "60 Minutes"?
25. Do you find yourself wanting more information after hearing a political speech?
26. Do you think a lot of advertising is false, an insult to your intelligence?
27. Do you occasionally think, "That was really dumb," after hearing other people talk?
28. Do you want to know how a machine, a watch, a violin, a jet airplane, really works?
29. Do you like watching the educational channel once in a while?
30. Do you like to read?
31. Do you ever read an encyclopedia just for the fun of it? Can you look up something and get sidetracked by all the interesting things you find?
32. Do you ever daydream about doing something no one else ever did?

33. Do you consider a lot of teenage fads dumb and a
    case of herd-following?

If you gave up to eleven yes answers you are possibly
gifted; up to twenty-two yes answers, probably gifted;
twenty-three or more, definitely gifted.

CHAPTER ◇ 16

What Is Your Gift?

Ll through grade school, junior high, and high school, nobody thought Houston was at all exceptional. He made average grades, tested middle of the road in just about everything. Fairly plain vanilla. Well liked, a good kid, enjoyed life, had a great sense of humor, but nobody visualized a brilliant future for him.

Houston had only one outstanding ability, and it was not one that anyone particularly noticed or considered worthwhile. Houston had an uncanny instinct for people— for what they were thinking, what was going on in their heads. Invariably he knew when his brothers and sisters were lying and usually the truth of whatever it was they were lying about.

When a new coach came to middle school and his sister Annie went out for the basketball team, Houston threw a fit. "Mom, don't let her do that," he pleaded. "There's something wrong with that guy. I think she'll be sorry."

Mother told him not to be silly, that she had met the coach and he seemed like a great guy. Annie tried out and made the team.

One day Houston came home from school and asked his mother to talk to Annie, saying that he knew something was wrong, something that involved the coach. Mom got halfway mad at Houston for being such a pain on the subject, but she decided it couldn't hurt to talk to her daughter.

She was horrified to learn that Annie was feeling very uneasy around the coach. He had a habit of walking into the girls' dressing room without knocking if he knew that only one or two girls were there. He would put his hand on a girl's shoulder and let the hand start to slide down, and he frequently made off-color jokes and remarks.

As far as Annie knew, he had not done anything that could get him jailed, but he couldn't seem to keep his hands to himself. Annie and the other girls felt it was only a matter of time before he did something really objectionable. Annie's parents talked with the parents of some of the other girls, and the end result was a meeting with school officials and the coach being asked to resign.

"How did you know?" Annie demanded of Houston. "I thought I was just imagining things or had a dirty mind or something. How did you know?"

Houston shrugged. "I don't know. I just did." And he didn't know. Almost by instinct, he had "read" the coach as the kind of man he was.

It didn't seem like a gift on which a career could be based, but a couple of years later a teacher noticed Houston's particular ability. When a particularly vicious act of vandalism had the school up in arms, the teacher suggested to the principal that he question the suspects, one at a time, with Houston in the room and then ask Houston who he thought was lying.

With Houston sitting in a corner with a hangdog expression as if he too were in trouble, the suspects were paraded through, and each fervently denied having anything to do with it. When the last was gone, Houston gave the principal two names and told him what he thought was behind the trouble.

Questioned more closely, the two admitted the vandalism and why they had committed it. Houston had hit it almost exactly dead center. And he knew what he wanted to do with his life.

Today he is a detective on the police force of a large West Coast city, the kind of detective of which legends are made. Another cop once commented that trying to lie to Houston was like "trying to hide a broken bone from an x-ray. He sees right through it."

With that kind of ability Houston might have gone into the mental health field in some capacity, or become a psychiatric nurse, or a great salesman. He could have done a number of things with great success, using his special gift.

Houston's unique ability did not show up in any of the school testing, and only one teacher had recognized it until the incident of the vandalism. Even afterward, few teachers considered it anything special. Yet it is taking Houston to the top of his chosen career field.

Laney had supurb eye-hand coordination. She was a whiz at sports like tennis and softball. Her home ec. teacher once joked that Laney could thread a sewing machine needle with the machine running. She was smart, but did not consider herself gifted in any way. She was also an adventurous girl who wanted to do something unusual in life. She didn't think she was good enough in sports to be a professional athlete. An uncle who was a doctor said she would make a good surgeon, but science didn't particularly interest her and she wasn't especially good in the courses that make up a pre-med curriculum.

During Career Day one year Laney was walking past the military recruiters when she was struck by something one of them was saying, and she stopped and edged closer to listen. The requirements for this job were just what Laney had—excellent coordination, especially eye-hand, good eyes, a sense of adventure. As Laney listened, becoming more and more interested and excited, she felt sure she had found what she wanted to do.

And she had. She became an Army helicopter pilot, one of the first American women to fly in combat in operation Desert Storm. She loved it—flying, the military life in general, the change and adventure of her job. Even being able to do one's job well in the face of danger brought a special satisfaction.

Laney's special ability, like Houston's, was not recognized or appreciated. Neither showed up on any standard test.

Certainly neither teenager was considered gifted, and yet both, in different ways, were exactly that.

Phil was positive that he was "just an average guy." He wasn't very athletic. He wasn't very handsome. He wasn't a brain. He never considered himself gifted. But he was popular.

He never really knew why, but everyone liked him, considered him a friend. The teachers liked him. The coach liked him. The gifted and talented kids liked him. The kids in the emotionally disturbed and learning dis-abled classes liked him. In fact, there was no one in shcool who didn't like him.

In spite of average looks, Phil had a sparkle, a zing, a zest for life, a rollicking sense of humor, a magnetism that everyone felt.

One day a director who specialized in radio and television commercials came to Phil's school to audition teens for a breakfast cereal commercial. Like everyone, he was impressed with Phil on first sight. Phil had a great screen test; the magnetism that everyone around him felt came right through the camera and onto the screen. Phil won a contract for the commercial. The rest, as they say, is history. Phil is still making commercials. He is also the wealthiest graduate his school ever had.

As we have said elsewhere, we believe that American schools, with their emphasis on standardization and categorizing, miss a lot that makes people gifted, especially if it is in just one area. So how do you find out what are your special strengths, even if you haven't tested out as "gifted and talented"?

There are a number of things you can do. Have you ever taken an aptitude test? These tests are not only interesting but a lot of fun, and they can tell you things about your abilities that can—and probably will—surprise you.

Some schools give aptitude tests routinely. In others they are available through the counselor's office, and in some they are not available at all. Even if your school falls into the last category, you can probably still arrange to take an aptitude test through a nearby vo-tech school or community college. Or call your state employment security commission. Such tests are routinely given to people drawing unemployment compensation in most states. If you cannot arrange to take a test there, someone can almost surely tell you where you can be tested.

Usually what you like is what you are good in, but it's a

sort of chicken-or-egg situation as to which comes first.

The best place to learn about the best use of your abilities is the library. Read about what you like to do best, and you will probably find an embarrassment of riches of ways to earn a good living doing just that.

Maybe you love, live, and breathe sports but can't see yourself as a good enough athlete to earn your living on a playing field or court. You don't have to be an athlete. You could become a coach or a sports reporter or writer. Maybe you could land an administrative job in the athletic department of a university or the management office of a professional team. You might become a technician, nurse, or doctor in a department of sports medicine, which is a rapidly growing branch of the medical field. Perhaps you could be a salesperson in sports equipment, or an architect who designs sports facilities such as swimming pools or stadiums.

Maybe you love and are good with horses. The horse industry is huge and full of well-paying jobs. Many colleges and universities offer programs in equine management that not only teach almost every aspect of the horse business but also help you find a job when you graduate.

Once you study the type of abilities you have and the best use of them, you are almost certain to find many career opportunities that are not apparent at first glance.

Don't feel that you have to be great at everything or that you have to be officially labeled as gifted. And don't let anyone pressure you into feeling that way, either.

Enjoy and plan to make the best use of the gifts you do have. They should be enough to assure you a successful and enjoyable life.

CHAPTER 17

"Lucky Breaks"

"Lucky breaks" are what happen when preparedness meets opportunity.

How often have you read or heard about someone—perhaps someone your age—who had gotten what looked like a great break in life and thought, "Some people have all the luck! Why in the blue-eyed world couldn't that have happened to me?"

The truth is, perhaps it did happen to you. Maybe somewhere along the line you got what you might have turned into a big break, but you either didn't recognize it or were not prepared to do anything with it.

Here are some case studies of young people who were prepared to make the most of breaks when they came.

Marti came from a terrible background. Her mother had serious health problems and was on medication that left her barely able to function. Her father had been injured in an oilfield accident when she was a baby. She didn't remember a time when the family wasn't on welfare.

Even so, Marti was an A student who was good at almost

anything she tried. Her favorite subject was history, especially the daily lives of famous people. She couldn't read enough about what they wore, ate, how they lived, what was and was not considered acceptable behavior. Her teachers had long since gotten over being surprised when she knew more about something than they did. Her hobby was drawing, sketching, and painting. She was good enough at it that art teachers urged her to make art her major in college.

"I can't," she told her high school counselor, and went on to explain. Her parents had surprised everyone by having twins, a boy and a girl, when Marti was thirteen and her mother almost fifty. With her parents' ages and state of health, Marti was being realistic. She knew she would probably have to finish raising and educating her brother and sister, and she needed a field that was more sure and steady than art, even commercial art. She went to college, on scholarships, and majored in history, planning to teach it.

In her first year in college, however, she saw a TV special set in Victorian times that was full of errors in the sets and costumes. She looked up the name of the prominent producers of the show, wrote to them pointing out some of the errors, and enclosed sketches of furnishings and costumes that would have been correct for the period. Then she put it out of her mind.

About three weeks later she got a telephone call from someone at the production company, asking how she knew all this. She told him, and they chatted for about half an hour. Three days later Marti received a letter from the company. They were doing a made-for-TV movie set along the Gulf Coast in 1928. Would she be interested in submitting some sketches? A dumbfounded Marti most certainly was interested.

A month passed and Marti, deep in studying for finals, had all but forgotten the matter when another letter came. The producers wanted to hire her as a set designer for this one movie. The salary nearly made her pass out cold.

"It's a hoax," she told her roommate. "There isn't that much money in the whole world."

Marti had no formal training in set design, but she dropped everything else, read everything the college library offered, talked to people in the drama department, and visited local TV stations with lists of questions.

When it was time to join the film company Marti was ready—on all counts. She knew, from thorough study, the history of the period to be represented, and she had the skills to make her part of the program work.

Today Marti works for that company and also free-lances in set and costume design, while finishing college part time. She commands a handsome salary, has moved her family into a better house, and knows she'll have no financial problems taking care of her brother and sister if the need should arise.

Marti got a lucky break. But she was gifted, multigifted. So she was also *prepared* to make the most of that break when it came.

Collette loved to cook. She was always puttering around the kitchen, and she especially liked to try new things, master more and more difficult recipes, and invent her own. Her friends counted themselves lucky when invited to Collette's for dinner, and her widowed mother, administrative assistant to a U.S. Senator, had no qualms about letting Collette do the cooking when she entertained important people.

One day a friend came to Collette at school with a copy

of a magazine. It contained an article about a recipe contest, and there was a junior division for anyone seventeen or under.

"Enter it," the friend urged. Collette did, and she won first prize of $5,000 and a trip to New York. A local TV station picked up the story and asked Collette to be their "guest chef," who cooked for the audience and the news crew on Fridays. Then a charity that held an annual dinner at which chefs from the city's best restaurants cooked (for $500 a plate!) invited Collette to be one of those chefs.

By now Collette's head was fairly reeling from the attention.

Three days after the charity dinner she received a call from the owner of the city's most exclusive hotel. He asked for an appointment and sent his limo for her. In his office, he said the hotel was always looking for someone with Collette's talent. What did she plan to do after high school?

Collette had always wanted to major in home economics, with emphasis on nutrition and food preparation, but her feminist mother had objected, saying that was too old-fashioned and urging Collette to plan a career "in this century, honey."

The hotel president said that after Collette graduated from high school—in about three months—they would be willing to sponsor her for a session at the world-famous Cordon Bleu cooking school in Paris, if she would agree to work for them for one year when she came home.

"I walked out of there pinching myself," she said. "It was like a dream coming true. A dream I'd always wanted, but didn't dare to even think about."

Collette leaves for Paris in a couple of weeks, and she has already started a notebook of plans for having a gourmet restaurant of her own someday.

When anyone asked Brad what he wanted to do when he grew up, he usually shrugged and said, "I guess be a lawyer like Dad," although he had no great interest in the law.

To himself he said, "You mean if Mom *lets* me grow up and doesn't work me to death." His mother was a passionate gardener who won top honors in flower shows and who early on enlisted Brad's help in the care of her garden.

He grumbled as a matter of routine, but he came to enjoy the work, even the physical heavy lifting and carrying that were part of it. He also found himself more and more interested in plants and how they grow in different settings.

Although he never yielded to his mother's urging to enter the shows himself ("Come *on*, Mom! Flowers! What would the guys say!"), he began to read books on plants and on landscaping, and when the family went on vacation he always wanted to visit botanical gardens, landscaped parks, and so on.

The summer after his sophomore year, the family moved to a new house, which in place of a lawn had about half an acre of raw, red earth. When his mother began to talk of planting this kind of flower here and that kind there, Brad rather hesitantly said, "Mom, I've got a better idea. Let's try this," and he showed her sketches he had made of how he would do the yard, with brick walls, fountains, even a Japanese meditation garden.

"I love it! It's wonderful," his mother said enthusiastically. "Unfortunately, I think your dad would stand on his head at the mere idea. After the house costing so much . . ."

But Brad had done his homework, scouting around, calling construction companies, especially those that specialized in urban renewal, and also wrecking companies. "A lot of things are available free just for hauling them away," he told her. Brad's father looked at the sketches and agreed, setting a figure below which the costs had to stay.

It took all summer and dozens of trips with a small trailer behind the car. Brad enlisted his friends, and his mom and older sister kept them fueled with pizza and pop. But by the end of the summer the lawn and back garden were done and it was a showplace. "People slowed down on the street to look," Brad said. "It gave me a lot of satisfaction."

The next spring the city held a "City Beautiful" contest, and Brad's design was awarded the top prize for a residence. He was all but stunned. A few weeks later he saw a small item in the newspaper: The city was asking for designs and bids for landscaping a public building under construction.

Brad was not sure how to go about it, so he asked questions. He found out the requirements for submitting a design and a bid for costs, and he won the contract. Again using his friends and what they had all learned the summer before (but this time everyone was being paid handsomely), Brad supervised a landscape design that was called one of the most beautiful in the city.

Brad doesn't even think about law now. He knows what his career is going to be after college, and he'll be going into it already having a string of awards and honors—and money.

Chris was bitten by the aviation bug (which bites with *authority*) at a very young age. "I think about three weeks," his mother often said. By the time Chris was ten he had his life planned. He wanted to go to college, major in aviation management, fly with the military, then go to the airlines. He also wanted to get his pilot's license the day he turned seventeen.

There was one major hitch to this, the kind everyone in aviation knows. There's a saying among pilots: If God had wanted men and women to fly, He'd have given us more money. Chris's father made a modest salary, and there were four other children in the family. Chris knew he would have to do it himself.

One day he rode his bike out to the airport, went into an office with Flight Instruction on the door, and asked what you had to do to become a pilot and how much it cost.

He went home, opened a savings account with the money in his piggy bank, and started asking neighbors if he could mow their lawns or wash their cars. Following the suggestion of the young man he had talked to at the airport, he went out there on weekends and asked if he could help wash and polish airplanes.

He requested money for every birthday and Christmas and never spent if he could help it. As soon as he was old enough he got a job in a fast-food restaurant. He became a family joke—"When it comes to money, Chris is tighter than the bark on a tree." But it paid off. He started flying lessons at the age of sixteen and a half and got his license one week after his seventeenth birthday.

When a young couple moved into the house next door, Chris was delighted to learn that the man was a pilot for an air freight company and that he sometimes flew air charters free-lance. Now and then, when insurance required it and no one else was available, Neal asked Chris to fly with him in the copilot's seat. Sometimes he even let Chris take the controls so he could log time. (The amount of flying time you have is crucial in many flying jobs.)

One evening Neal called Chris and asked him to come

over and bring his log book. After looking at it for a while and adding up hours, he said, "A number of times I've had to pass up flights because no copilot was available. The company I fly for most often is going to have an opening for a part-time pilot in about a month. You have almost enough hours to meet the insurance requirement. And you're a *good* pilot.

"You know you can't be hired you until you have a commercial rating, and to fly their twin engine planes you'd need a multiengine. If you had those I'd recommend that they hire you, and I think they'd do it on my say-so. Is there any way you could get them?"

Once again it was a matter of money, but Chris merely said, "I'll *make* a way." Using his car as collateral, and pointing out his record of making and saving money starting when he was twelve, Chris got a bank loan to cover the cost of the training he needed.

He celebrated the start of his senior year by being hired part time by the air charter company. While his friends spend weekends flipping hamburgers or sacking groceries, Chris is flying a Cessna 414 taking millionaires on ski vacations, flying blood or organs for medical use, or transporting machinery to remote towns to be picked up for oil drilling rigs.

"At this point, I'd say my life is about five years ahead of schedule," he says. "And you can't believe how much I love what I'm doing."

Growing up on the tough side of Tulsa, Susan Eleanor Hinton loved to read. But she had a problem: Most adult books were too adult for her, and most of the books for teens were about girls competing for and "getting" boys, which she found boring. "So I started writing a book, mainly so I'd have something to read." Published when she was seventeen, *The Outsiders* became an instant classic; it is required reading all over the country and was made into a movie and a TV series.

To a lot of kids it probably seems that these teens had "lucky breaks." And they did. What fell in their laps was good fortune in the form of opportunity. What they contributed to the formula was preparedness. All had focused on what they wanted to do and worked to hone and polish and expand that skill or that knowledge, even when—as in Chris's case—it cost time and money. Kids who thought Chris was a real nerd then are now the color of lime Jello with envy when on Saturday mornings they head for a job at the fast-food joint and he is heading to the airport to fly to New York or Mexico or Canada.

Let's get personal. Following are the authors' versions of their own lucky breaks, less spectacular than some, but things that made a difference in our lives.

Dr. Clayton talking now. My car broke down in Ft. Worth, Texas, in June of 1969, and I didn't have enough money to get it repaired. So I went to an employment office to get a job. The Veterans Administration man there asked to see my discharge papers. I told him I was looking for a laborer's job, but he said, "With a service record like this, you should be in management." I laughed, but he got me a job in management. It made a great difference in my life.

In 1976 I received a Dean's Award scholarship to attend Emory University basically free, to work on a master's degree. I couldn't have gone without the award. Everyone kept saying, "You're the luckiest guy I know."

Lucky? For four years I had been pastoring two churches

and driving 100 miles each way to college. I recorded lectures and listened to them as I drove. I studied late into the night every night. I graduated with a 3.83 average— only five Bs. Luck had nothing to do with it.

In 1981 I left the ministry to become executive director of a mental health clinic. Lucky? No way. I had taken courses in counseling while working for my master's degree, and I went to school after completing the degree to take additional courses in counseling. I had completed over half of a doctoral degree in counseling. How did I get so lucky? I didn't. I paid my dues first. Then I got the job. That's how you "get lucky."

My acquaintances still say, "He's such a lucky guy." My friends say, "He's one of the hardest workers I know." They're right.

Sharon Carter here. My "lucky break" was less spectacular than most, but it made a radical difference in my life.

One day I ran across the man who had taught me to fly, who was then a corporate pilot. We chatted a while, and as I turned to go he said casually, "You like to write stories about aviation. There's a guy who hangars a plane where we keep ours who's really interesting. He's an airshow pilot, and I'll bet you could get a good story out of him."

I was always interested in a good story, particularly about flying, so I made a note of the name and telephone number.

It lay in my desk for about a week while I was wrapped up in other things, but finally I called the man and made an appointment.

I walked into an office at the appointed tme to meet a man a shade shorter than I, with a ready grin, a personable manner, and an engaging laugh—half sheepish, as if he couldn't understand why anyone would want to interview him, and half as if the fame he was beginning to enjoy was a huge joke.

I said, "Is your name really Tom Jones?" Like most people, I was thinking of the book, or the Welsh singer.

He laughed. "It is. At least no one forgets it."

We talked a bit, and he told me about a spectacular crash he had had two years earlier. Before an airshow crowd his engine had blown apart and he had plunged through the roof of a hanger—and walked away from the wreck. I was bug-eyed. I knew this guy was going to be worth more than just one story.

Then he mentioned competition aerobatic flying. I didn't know such a thing existed. "Oh, yes," he said casually. "I belong to an aerobatics club. Why don't you come to our next meeting?"

To make a long story somewhat shorter, I wrote and had published a long string of stories about Tom. I joined the aerobatics club and have been an active member ever since. Recently I became an International Aerobatics Club fully qualified judge. I made a lot of good friends through that club, the Okie Twisters. A story I wrote about them, and Tom, appeared in the *New York Times*.

Tom became the National Aerobatics Champion in 1988. He flew before an estimated five million people in the United States and Canada. He became the most sought after airshow pilot in America.

I was there when Tom and another Oklahoma Aviation Hall of Famer, Ted Stranzyck, gathered a bunch of us aviation people together at the Air Space Museum and said, "Hey, folks, lets have a *real* airshow in Oklahoma City."

That airshow was Aerospace America. In three years we were the fifth largest airshow in the United States. By our fourth year we were recognized by the industry itself as the best airshow in the country. Working on it, being a part of it, was exhausting and exciting and exhilarating—the high point of one's year.

Aerospace America '90 made international history. That year the Soviet Union's AN-225, the largest airplane in the world, was shown outside the USSR for only the third time. Well before eight in the morning, a crowd had gathered to watch it land in Oklahoma City.

But the real history came two days later when two Sukhoi Su-27 Flanker fighters crossed over into Alaska en route to Oklahoma. It was the first time Soviet fighters had been permitted into U.S. airspace. It was with a feeling of complete unreality that I, very much a child of the Cold War, watched airplanes with red stars on their tails fly against a blue Oklahoma sky.

If anyone had ever told me I'd one day be standing in the Myriad Gardens in Oklahoma City hugging a Russian fighter pilot, I'd have said he was crazy. But that is what happened.

I cried all over one the next day—when Tom crashed and was killed in front of more than 70,000 people.

That chance meeting changed so much of my life. Many people came to know me through what I wrote about Tom. I made a lot of friends through the Twisters and working on the airshow. I was there, not just seeing it, but part of it, when history was made. I got to meet and came to like a number of those "alien" creatures—Russians.

It was luck that might easily never have happened. But when it did I was prepared. I had spent years honing my writing skills and learning all I could about aviation. When Tom said, "Come take an aerobatic flight with me," I had the nerve to do it and the ability to write about it in a way he said, "came out a sort of poetry."

For Further Reading

Arnold, Allyn. *Secondary Program for the Gifted and Talented*. Ventura, CA: Ventura County Superintendent of Schools Office, 1981.

Clark, Barbara. *Growing Up Gifted*. Columbus, OH: Merrill, 1978.

Clendening, Corinne. *Creating Programs for the Gifted: Teacher's, Parent's and Student's Guide*. New York: R. R. Bowker Company, 1980.

Daniels, Paul. *The Gifted/Learning Disabled Child*. Rockville, MD: Aspen Systems, 1983.

Galbraith, Judy. *The Gifted Kids' Survival Guide*. Minneapolis: Free Spirit Press, 1983.

Green, Lawrence. *Kids Who Underachieve*. New York: Simon & Schuster, 1986.

Haladyna, Thomas. *Instruments for the Identification of the Gifted, with Emphasis on the Economically Disadvantaged*. Seattle: Northwest Clearinghouse for Gifted Education, 1982.

Lawless, Ruth. *The Gifted Potential in Special Education Students*. Seattle: Northwest Clearinghouse for Gifted Education, 1982.

Miller, Bernard, and Price, Merle, eds. *The Gifted Child, the Family, and the Community*. New York: American Association for Gifted Children, 1981.

Moore, Linda. *Does This Mean My Kid's a Genius?* New York: McGraw-Hill, 1981.

Reynolds, Ben. *Writing Instruction for Verbally Talented Youth: The Johns Hopkins Model*. Rockville, MD: Aspen Systems, 1984.

Sellin, Donald. *Educating Gifted and Talented Learners*. Rockville, MD: Aspen Systems, 1980.

Treffinger, Donald. *Encouraging Creative Learning for the Gifted and Talented*. Ventura, CA: Ventura County Superintendent of Schools Office, 1980.

Tuttle, Frederick. *Characteristics and Identification of Gifted and Talented Students*. Washington, DC: National Education Association, 1980.

Van Tassel-Basko, Joyce, ed. *A Practical Guide to Counseling the Gifted in a School Setting*. Reston, VA: Council for Exceptional Children, 1983.

Whitmore, Joanne. *Giftedness, Conflict, and Underachievement*. Boston: Allyn and Bacon, 1980.

Index